NIGHT OF THE
BLACK BEAR

A MYSTERY IN GREAT SMOKY MOUNTAINS NATIONAL PARK

GLORIA SKURZYNSKI AND ALANE FERGUSON

NATIONAL
GEOGRAPHIC
WASHINGTON, D.C.

To Jacob Matthew Ronald Ledesma,

the newest member of our family.

Text copyright © 2007 Gloria Skurzynski and Alane Ferguson
Cover illustration copyright © 2007 Jeffrey Mangiat

For information about bulk purchases, please contact National Geographic Books
Special Sales, ngspecsales@ngs.org

Map by Carl Mehler, Director of Maps
Map research and production by Sven M. Dolling

Black bear art by Ruthie Thompson, Thunderhill Graphics

This is a work of fiction. Any resemblance to living persons or events other than
descriptions of natural phenomena is purely coincidental.

Library of Congress Cataloging-in-Publication Data available on request.

ISBN 978-1-4263-0094-3 (paperback)
ISBN 978-1-4263-0105-6 (Library)

Printed in the United States of America

ACKNOWLEDGMENTS

The authors want to thank Steve Kemp,

the Interpretive Products & Services Director for

Great Smoky Mountains Association;

Kent Cave, the Interpretive Media Branch Chief at

Great Smoky Mountains National Park;

Kim DeLozier, the Supervisory Wildlife Biologist at

Great Smoky Mountains National Park; and

Jan Skurzynski, who wrote the songs

Merle sings in this book.

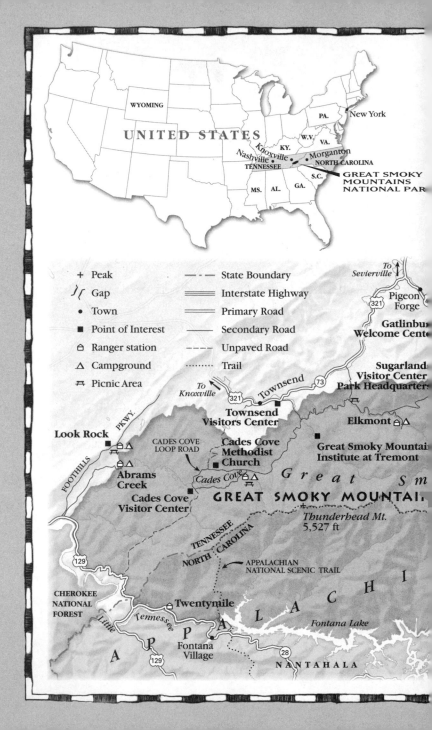

United States Map:

WYOMING

UNITED STATES

New York
PA.
W.V. VA.
KY.
Knoxville
Nashville
TENNESSEE
Morganton
NORTH CAROLINA
S.C.
GREAT SMOKY
MOUNTAINS
NATIONAL PARK
MS. AL. GA.

Legend:

+ Peak
)(Gap
• Town
■ Point of Interest
⌂ Ranger station
△ Campground
⊟ Picnic Area

— · — State Boundary
═══ Interstate Highway
══ Primary Road
— Secondary Road
---- Unpaved Road
········ Trail

Park Map labels:

To Sevierville

Pigeon Forge
321

Gatlinburg
Welcome Center

Sugarland
Visitor Center
Park Headquarters

To Knoxville
321
73
Townsend

Townsend
Visitors Center

Elkmont ⌂△

Look Rock

PKWY.

FOOTHILLS

CADES COVE
LOOP ROAD

Cades Cove
Methodist
Church

Great Smoky Mountains
Institute at Tremont

⌂△
Abrams
Creek

Cades Cove ⌂△

Cades Cove
Visitor Center

G r e a t   S m

GREAT SMOKY MOUNTAIN

Thunderhead Mt.
5,527 ft

129

TENNESSEE
NORTH CAROLINA

APPALACHIAN
NATIONAL SCENIC TRAIL

CHEROKEE
NATIONAL
FOREST

Twentymile

Little

Tennessee

A   P   P   A   L   A   C   H   I

Fontana Lake

129

Fontana
Village

28

NANTAHALA

GREAT SMOKY MOUNTAINS NATIONAL PARK

States: North Carolina and Tennesee

Established: 1934

Area: 520,409 acres (210,602 ha)

Name Origin: The "smoky" haze that gives the mountains and park their names is caused by sunlight interacting with water vapor and plant hydrocarbons.

Features: World-famous for its diversity of plants and animals (1,500 varieties of flowering plants, some 1,400 black bears, 200 bird species, and 30 kinds of salamanders), more than 800 miles of trails, and its open-air museum of southern Appalachian mountain life

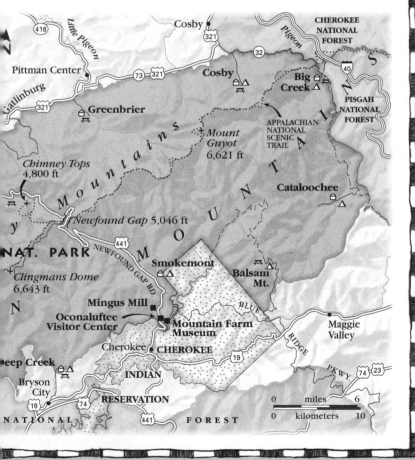

The man liked to stack bills neatly. Ten-dollar bills on top of tens, their edges in a straight line, with separate stacks for the twenties and the fifties and the hundreds. Tonight there were seven hundred-dollar bills—pretty good earnings, he thought, in spite of the TV report that had scared some of his clients. Scared them, but excited them at the same time—five new clients had made reservations for tomorrow night. His pile of money would grow fatter still.

He'd begun to count the twenties and tens when his phone rang, and he hesitated. To answer, or not to answer? It was after hours, so the business was supposed to be closed for the night, but it could be another client, which meant more crisp bills to add to his pile.

"Yeah," he spoke briskly into the phone. "Oh, yeah, Mr. Cabelli, I've been watching the reports. She wasn't killed, just sliced and diced a bit. No, she was bloodied up, but that's all. Don't worry about our end. All systems are go."

Through the window he saw a car edge into the parking lot near his office. A white car, with the words

PARK RANGER and a green horizontal stripe above the front fender. It eased past the window like a shark gliding through water. Probably meant nothing, but—

"I gotta go, Mr. Cabelli."

Quietly the man put down the phone and switched off the office lights. Then, with nothing but the soft glow of his watch to guide him, he placed the money in a bulging blue bag and zipped it shut.

Blood or no blood, he had work to do. He slipped out the side door of his office, locked the bag in the trunk of his black Town Car, and drove away into the night.

NIGHT OF THE BLACK BEAR

CHAPTER ONE

J ack was stunned to see the blood on the ground.
Deep red, it had seeped into the tall grass behind
one of the tombstones, arcing like a fan until it
sank into a bare patch of earth. A small, trench-like
depression showed where the bear had dragged
the girl. Jack had heard that a tourist scared away the
bear, making it run off into the trees beyond the cemetery.
The girl, the bear's victim, had been lucky to escape alive.
Sometimes a black bear will hold on so tight that nothing
can make it drop its prey.

It seemed really weird to have a cemetery in a U.S.
national park—as far as Jack knew, this was the only one.
But long before Great Smoky Mountains National Park
came into existence, people had lived here. They farmed
and hunted wild turkeys, deer, and black bears. When they
died, they were buried right where Jack was standing.

Walking carefully, he tried not to step on any of the
blood. Some drops still clung to the leaves of the yellow
lady's slippers that reached up like tiny cupped hands
toward the midday sun. He leaned closer, his fingers

cautiously touching the tip of a bloody leaf to see if the blood was still wet. It was! Grimacing, he wiped his fingers on his khaki cargo shorts.

From around the side of the white-walled Cades Cove Methodist Church his sister Ashley called out, "Mom says Heather's going to be OK."

"Who's Heather? Is she the girl the bear attacked?"

"Yes, Heather McDonald is her name," Ashley answered him. "Anyway, she's going to be all right. Mom talked to the park ranger at the hospital, and he told her Heather will probably be discharged tomorrow." She squinted up at Jack. "What's the matter? You look— grossed out or something."

"Nothing's the matter. I'm fine," Jack told her, regretting that he had wiped his fingers on his shorts, which were now stained with a bloody reminder of the bear attack.

"OK, well, Mom said she'll be just a bit longer, and then we can go." Ashley zipped up her pink hoodie, shivering a little. Though it was nearly May, the air felt a bit chilly.

Jack glanced across the churchyard toward his mother. Olivia Landon was a wildlife veterinarian, who frequently was called to various national parks as a consultant when- ever there were strange, unexplained happenings with the animals. A small woman with curly dark hair—Ashley got her looks from their mother—Olivia was deep in conversation with a uniformed park ranger, Blue Firekiller, a tall, muscular man with black hair and skin the color of pale copper. They were questioning a bald-headed man who had witnessed the attack. As they spoke together, Ranger Firekiller wrote in a small notebook while the man waved his hands and gestured toward the trees.

A little farther away, Jack's father, Steven Landon, changed the film in his camera, while talking to a tall boy who had the same copper skin and black hair as Ranger Blue Firekiller. "Who's that kid over there with Dad?" Jack asked Ashley.

With a slight smile, Ashley answered, "That's Ranger Firekiller's son. His name is Yonah. He told me he's a Cherokee, and Firekiller is a real Cherokee name. So is Yonah."

There was something about Ashley's smile and the way she said "Yonah" that caught Jack's attention. "What's so special about him?" he asked.

"It's just—you know how I always collect Native American legends at every park we go to. Yonah was telling me all about the bear trouble today, and he said something I can really connect to. He said he understood what the bear was feeling."

"What the bear was *feeling?* You mean the bear that attacked the girl right over there? This Yonah sounds kind of weird to me, like he's been reading *Goldilocks* or something."

Defiant, Ashley glared at her brother, redness creeping into her cheeks. Little wisps of hair curled from her dark braids, tiny as threads, and in the light they seemed to spark in aggravation. "Jack, I'm 12 years old—almost!" she hissed. "Do you think Yonah would be telling me fairy tales like I was a little kid? We had a serious conversation. Just because I'm two years younger than you doesn't mean a 16-year-old guy won't talk to me about serious things."

"I know what the bear was feeling, too," Jack told her. "He was feeling hungry."

"Shut up!" Ashley punched him in the arm.

Jack narrowed his eyes to study Yonah, who was tall and wiry, with biceps that bulged as he stood with his arms across his chest. Yonah seemed to be listening intently to the talk between the three adults while at the same time paying attention to what Steven was doing with his camera.

"Anyway, I'll introduce you to him," Ashley told Jack, making it sound like a big favor. "Hey, Yonah!" she called, waving her arm to catch his attention. "Can you come here a minute? My brother wants to meet you."

"Not," Jack muttered.

Yonah glanced from his dad to Olivia to Steven, shrugged, then sauntered to where Jack and Ashley were standing. Through holes in his blue jeans, his knees looked like flickering eyes as he walked, and his thick bangs hung to his eyebrows in a line so straight it might have been drawn with a ruler. "Yeah?" he asked.

"This is Jack," Ashley said. "Jack, this is Yonah. I was telling Jack what you said about the bear, Yonah, but I thought you could say it better."

"How do you spell Yonah?" Jack asked.

Yonah paused after each letter, as though Jack might not be swift enough to catch it. "'Yonah' means 'bear.'"

"So that's how you know what bears are thinking—you *are* one!" Jack started to laugh at his own little joke, but no one else was laughing. Yonah's face stayed expressionless. His dark eyes skimmed over Jack's blond hair, blue eyes, and pale skin with a look that told Jack he could never qualify as a Cherokee.

For some reason that silent stare flustered Jack. He found himself doing the thing he chided his sister for—he began to talk too fast. "My mom – she's Olivia Landon, the wildlife veterinarian. She's over there with your dad. She came here to confer about the elk, and then this bear thing happened, so now she's helping them figure out the science of why the bears have gone haywire." Jack rushed on, "We were driving from the airport this morning when we got the phone call about this attack, so we came straight over here. My mom nearly freaked out when she heard there'd been a total of three bear incidents in the past four weeks. This is a really serious situation. She said—"

"Two," Yonah interrupted.

The tone stopped Jack cold. "Excuse me?"

"One of the attacks was in Gatlinburg, which is out-side the park. Heather McDonald is only the second victim in Great Smoky Mountains National Park. It's important to keep the facts straight, especially if the media show up."

Feeling quashed, Jack stood silent, unsure what Yonah meant. Overhead, a magpie cawed, and beyond that he could hear a car rumble past on Cades Cove Loop Road, a good distance beyond the thick stands of trees that ringed the wide green meadow around the Methodist church. He felt stupid standing there without answering, but he didn't know what to say.

"Do you really think the news people will show up, Yonah?" Ashley asked.

"You can pretty much count on it. They like to ask questions that make things sound worse than they are." Although Ashley had questioned him, Yonah directed his answer at Jack. "My dad—he's the ranger that got called in to investigate the attacks—he told me if we're not care-ful, the media people might try to shut down Great Smoky Mountains National Park. So watch what you say. And how you say it. Don't go blabbing stupid stuff."

Jack found his voice and said, "Yeah, well, my mom's more worried about somebody getting killed. She thinks that's the bigger problem."

"Black bears don't kill," Yonah replied. "Not unless they are provoked."

"You mean like Heather provoked that bear by standing here in the cemetery?" Jack shot back. If he hadn't been sure before, he was sure of it now—he didn't much like this guy. Ashley stood to one side, glancing from one to the other of them anxiously as she rocked from foot to foot, her dark eyes wide.

"These attacks are very unusual," Yonah continued. "It's just a string of bad luck."

"Yeah, you're right. Especially for the people who get chunks of their thighs ripped open. That's really bad luck."

"Jack!"

"What?" Jack cried, whirling on his sister.

"Look! Over there."

For an instant he thought she was telling him to cool it with Yonah, but instead, Ashley pointed to the road, where two vans, one with something like a radar scope on the roof, were turning onto the blacktop lane that led to the church. Within minutes the vans arrived and parked, then their doors flew open.

Three people got out and rushed toward the spot where Olivia, Steven, and Blue Firekiller stood talking to a bald-headed man. A young blonde-haired woman in a red blazer, short skirt, and knee-high boots led the group. A man beside her balanced a television camera on his shoulder. Another man behind them carried a long pole with a microphone dangling from it.

"I'm Greta Gerard from Channel 12 News," the woman announced, as the man with the pole thrust the microphone a half dozen inches from Blue's face. "We understand there's been another bear attack in the park, this one almost fatal. Can you give us some details?"

Yonah had begun to hurry back toward his father, and Jack and Ashley followed in time to hear Greta Gerard ask, "What is the park's position on these attacks, Mr....?" Then, peering at Blue's nametag, "I mean Ranger...uh... Firekiller? Is that right? Firekiller?"

Suddenly, Yonah spoke up, saying, "Yes, the name is Firekiller. It's Cherokee."

"Firekiller, OK, got it," Greta murmured, barely glancing at Yonah. "So, Ranger Firekiller, what does the park have to say about these attacks? Will you be forced to close the park to the public?"

Hesitating, Blue Firekiller answered, "A black bear did approach a girl visiting here in Cades Cove, but we're happy to report that she's doing fine."

"'Approach?' That's an interesting choice of words," Greta answered. "I heard it was an attack. Some of the tourists I have talked to have asked if the bears in this park might have rabies. Do you think that's possible? An outbreak of rabies could threaten the public's health and safety."

"No. In the other incidents the tests all came back negative," Blue replied as he frowned at Greta. His right hand twitched as though he wanted to brush away the microphone that kept inching closer to his face.

"Well, then, Ranger Firekiller, do you have any explanation as to why the black bears are behaving in such an unusual manner?" Greta signaled the cameraman to focus on her, rather than on Blue. "Our viewers will want to know, just how far will Great Smoky Mountains National Park go to protect the visitors who come here? After all, this is the most visited national park in the entire United States National Park System."

"We have no evidence whatsoever that the bears are infected with any disease," Blue told her, holding himself stiffly. "But we're taking the situation very seriously. We've asked Dr. Landon, an expert on animal behavior who just happens to be visiting the park, to help us study every possible scenario."

Suddenly the bald man, who'd been standing quietly through all this, stepped forward to announce, "I saw the whole thing. I'm the guy who saved the girl." He pushed in front of Blue to be in line with the camera while he added, "That bear was acting crazy. I heard the girl yell, and I knew I had to save her. My name is William F. Jordan. That's spelled J-o-r-d-a-n."

"Are you the bear expert?" Greta asked him.

"Me? No." He shook his head. "That lady over there—

she's the bear expert. Anyway, like I told the lady and Ranger Firekiller here, I heard the girl screaming, and I ran over to her. I'd just come out of the church 'cause my wife left her scarf there this morning, and—"

"The bear," Greta prompted him, "tell us about the bear."

"Well, I ran over there, and I yelled and clapped my hands, then I picked up a rock and threw it. My pitching arm is still pretty good. The rock hit the bear right on his head. *Bonk!* He kind of roared, like he was gonna come after me, but then he ran into the trees behind the cemetery. Seems like all the bears in this park have gone crazy. Three maulings already—"

"Two!" Yonah spoke up.

"They need to shut down this park to protect the American people," Jordan insisted.

"Will that be the official park position?" Greta asked, ignoring both Yonah and Mr. Jordan as she turned back toward Blue. "To close the park?"

Olivia had begun to inch away from the camera while Greta's attention focused on Blue, who pulled himself up to his imposing six-foot height before he answered, "We have no further comment. If you have any more questions, Miss, you'll need to talk to the park superintendent."

"But did you see the girl who was attacked?" Greta persisted. "I heard the bear ripped a whole pound of flesh out of her leg."

"No comment!"

"Dr. Landon? What's your opinion?"

"I can't even begin to speculate until I go over the data," Olivia said, signaling Jack and Ashley to head toward the Landons' rental car. Ashley, fascinated by the television news team, barely moved, so Jack jerked her by the elbow to get her going. Steven followed, pulling out the car keys as he herded the kids forward, their feet scuffing against the asphalt. As if by magic, the car doors flew open, all four at once.

The camera zoomed in as Greta cried, "Dr. Landon, do you think it's in the public's best interest to shut down Great Smoky Mountains National Park?"

"Ranger Firekiller has already told you that you'll need to discuss that with the park superintendent," Olivia answered.

Steven had started the car and was easing it toward the TV crew, with the front passenger door still wide open. Suddenly, Olivia sprinted across the last ten feet that separated her from the car and jumped inside without saying another word. The engine roared as Steven shifted into reverse, spun in a curve and swung back onto the road, leaving Greta standing there, frustrated.

"Wow! That was a real cool escape, Mom!" Jack exclaimed.

Olivia swept her fingers through her hair, squeezed her eyes shut, and took a deep breath before she answered, "That Greta person kept clamoring about closing the park, and I bet it'll be all over the television news tonight. We have to solve this mystery so that we can keep the park open. What I really need is to interview that girl, Heather McDonald. And I need to get to her now!"

CHAPTER TWO

Blue and Yonah managed to slide into their own car and race after the Landons. As they caught up, Blue honked his horn to signal that he was passing, then swung ahead on the left as Yonah yelled through his passenger-side window, "Follow us to the hospital."

"Thank heavens for Blue!" Olivia exclaimed. "I never got a chance to find out where the hospital's located."

Both cars slowed down to head out on the long drive. As their parents talked quietly in the front seat, Jack and Ashley stared out the rear windows at the sights. And there were a lot of sights to see, especially when they reached the town of Pigeon Forge, Tennessee. Streets that looked like an amusement park were lined with tourist attractions, one after the other, competing for the attention of passersby. Jack sat up straight when he realized that there actually *was* an amusement park, a real one, hardly more than a stone's throw beyond the main highway.

Ashley beat him to it. She shouted out, "Dollywood! Look, there's a sign for Dollywood. It says rides and a water park. Mom, can we go there?"

"Probably. Eventually. After we've taken care of the bear problem." Jack noticed his mother biting the edge of her thumbnail and figured she must be seriously worried. He'd never seen her bite her nails before. "At the hospital, kids," she added, "we'll be meeting a ranger named Kip Delaney. Kip is the park's expert on the elk restoration program, but he's also a black bear expert. I've talked to him on the phone in the past hour, and we're both thinking there could be some remote tie-in between the bear attacks and the elk. I mean, that's really just a guess, but Kip and I want to investigate it."

Kip Delaney. These park guys have funny names, Jack thought. Blue, Yonah, Kip....

Fifteen minutes later they pulled into the hospital parking lot in a town called Sevierville. Kip Delaney was outside waiting for them, motioning them into a space he'd saved. Like Blue Firekiller, Kip Delaney was tall and dark-haired, but Kip had fair skin, and his shoulders were so broad that when he reached out to shake hands, his gray, park ranger shirt pulled tight across his chest.

"Looks like everyone's here," Kip said.

Yonah and Blue had arrived just ahead of the Landons, and Blue was saying, "We need gas. The gauge is nearly on empty." Holding out the car keys, he told Yonah, "Here, take Jack and Ashley with you, gas up the car, and then buy yourselves some burgers if you're hungry. Come back in about half an hour."

Hearing that, it was Steven, not Olivia, who began to look worried. "Yonah has his license?" he asked, as if he didn't really want to trust his kids to a 16-year-old he'd just met that afternoon.

"Sure. I've been legal for a whole month," Yonah told him confidently. "Don't worry, Mr. Landon, I'm a very careful driver. I promise I won't go over 80. Just joking. Anyway, the gas station and burger place are only two blocks from here."

Ashley giggled a little at Yonah's joke, but Jack shook his head and said, "I'm not hungry."

"Well, I'm starving!" Ashley declared, shooting a look at Jack.

"Since when are you not hungry?" Steven asked him. "The last time you weren't hungry, you were eight years old and had chickenpox."

The truth was, Jack already didn't like Yonah very much and would rather not be stuck with him for half an hour. Besides, if he stayed around the hospital, he might learn more about Heather McDonald and the bear encounter. That would really be interesting.

"If you stay, you'll have to wait in the hall," Olivia told him. "You can't go into the room."

"Fine. No problem." Jack didn't bother to wave as Yonah and Ashley took off.

"Let's go, then," Kip said, and led the rest of them toward Heather McDonald's hospital room. Blue entered first, followed by Olivia, Steven, and Kip. As they went in, Jack tried to get a glimpse inside, but with all those adults filling the door frame, he couldn't see a thing. Then Kip shut the door tightly behind him.

"Perfect!" Jack grumbled sarcastically. He glanced around the hall and saw some empty chairs. A small square table held a few magazines, but he had no desire to read *Quilter's Digest* or *Healthy Aging* or *Cooking for Vegans*. He sprawled on one of the chairs, resting the back of his head against the wall. A nurse who happened to come out of Heather's room did not shut the door tightly. After she disappeared down the hall, Jack jumped to his feet and moved toward the door, which had swung open a couple of inches. That was enough.

Staying back a little so he wouldn't be quite up against the opening, Jack peered first at the girl in the hospital bed. Heather's eyes looked wide and shadowed, her face pasty pale, and her colorless lips quivered as the adults questioned her.

"…with our church group," she was saying. "I went out to the cemetery because my dad told me some of our ancestors are supposed to be buried there. I wanted to find the tombstones."

"Were your parents with the church group?" Olivia asked gently.

"No, they stayed home. In Morganton. That's where we're from—Morganton, North Carolina. It's about 150 miles from here. But my mom's here now." Heather's lips trembled even more as two tears slid down her cheeks.

Heather's mother, sitting somewhere Jack couldn't see, said, "I came as soon as they called me this morning."

The sad-looking girl in the hospital bed was about 16, Jack guessed, the same age as Yonah. Her bandaged leg lay on top of the bedding, but the rest of her thin body stayed beneath the white hospital sheets. Greta, the TV newswoman, had claimed that a pound of flesh had been torn from Heather's thigh, yet there was no way to tell how deep the wound was because of those thick bandages covering Heather's leg from her hip to below the knee.

Jack's father must have been standing in a corner behind the door. Jack couldn't see him but heard him ask Heather's mother, "Do I have your permission to take a few photos for the park reports?"

Mrs. McDonald murmured, "Yes," and there was a sudden flash from Steven's camera. Heather blanched as the camera flashed two more times.

"So you found the tombstones, Heather," Olivia went on, "and then what did you do?"

"I put down my backpack—"

"Did you have food in your backpack?" Olivia interrupted.

"Uh-huh. I had a chicken sandwich on a wheat bagel. And some potato chips."

Jack could see his mother exchange a glance with Kip, but Olivia asked only, "What happened next, Heather?"

"Well, I started to take pictures of the tombstones. With my digital camera. It's over there in the drawer, if you want to see it."

"Maybe later," Kip said. Then, raising his hands to his face as though holding a camera, he continued, "When you took the pictures, did you have the camera up like this? Near your face?"

"Well, yes, I was holding it up to see the little screen— you know, that shows what the picture will look like? I guess, I suppose…it was in front of my face."

Kip took a deep breath. "Then this might be what caused the attack. The bear probably thought you were eating something, Heather. First, he smelled the food in your backpack. Bears have a powerful sense of smell," Kip explained to Heather's mother. "Even from way back in the woods, bears can smell food a mile away. When he came close and saw you holding your camera up near your face, he thought the camera was food, and he wanted it. So what did you do then?"

"Well…I…" Heather glanced down, glanced away, ran her fingers through her tangled brown hair. "I guess I did something really stupid. I took pictures of the bear."

"Oh…my!" Blue breathed. He'd been writing in the small notebook, but now he paused, his pen raised, as he looked over at Heather.

"Like I said, it was stupid...a huge mistake. *Huge!*"
Heather cried, her voice breaking as she began to sob.
"I know that now! Because the bear came at me and he
tried to grab the camera and I started hitting him with it
and he bit me on the leg. I screamed, but he kept biting
me, and I kept screaming, and then this man came and—"

"It's all right, Heather, we know the rest of it from the
report you gave to Ranger Delaney." Olivia pressed her
hand lightly against the girl's cheek, trying to soothe her.
"And we talked to the man who saved you."

"Excuse me!" The words came from right behind Jack
and made him jump. He whirled around to see a white-
coated woman with a stethoscope sticking out from her
pocket. "I need to get in this room," she said.

"Oh, sorry!" Jack moved out of the way as the woman
pushed through the door, leaving it even farther ajar.

"I'm Dr. Graham. You wanted to talk to me?" she
asked Kip.

Kip nodded and moved back so the doctor could
come closer to Heather's bed. "We'll need a description
of Heather's wound for our report, Doctor. Can you tell
us about it—in layman's language, please, so Ranger
Firekiller here knows how to spell the words?" Kip threw
a quick grin at Blue.

The doctor didn't smile at all. In a clipped voice that
sounded as though she had other emergencies waiting
for her and she couldn't spare too much time, she said,

"I anesthetized the wound and examined it to see how deep it was. Then I debrided it."

"De-breed?" Blue asked, raising his pen from the pad and scrunching up his brow. "What does that mean?"

"It means to cut away some of the damaged tissue."

"You cut away more tissue?" Now Blue's eyebrows lifted way up. "She already had this big hole in her leg. Why didn't you just stitch it up?"

Impatiently the doctor said, "It's difficult to stitch animal bites. By definition they are contaminated. Making sutures—you call them stitches—would be like leaving foreign bodies inside the wound—a perfect place for infection to localize. Bear saliva is very germy. But we were able to check for rabies, and the results came back negative. No rabies, so that's good news."

The doctor's tone changed as she leaned over Heather to ask, "Feeling any better, honey? The pain pills and antibiotics ought to be helping." Then, straightening, the doctor turned toward Olivia. "She'll need plastic surgery to repair the wound, but her mother prefers to take her to the family's own physicians in North Carolina, isn't that right, Mrs. McDonald? Heather will be fit to travel by tomorrow." Giving Heather's hand a squeeze, the doctor told her, "I have to go now, sweetie, but I'll back to check on you later, after all these people are gone."

"Thanks for your time, Doctor," Kip said.

"You're welcome. By the way, who is that boy lurking around the door?"

Busted! Jack backed off fast, but not fast enough. It was Blue who came out to tell him, "Look, Jack, we're still going to be here for a while, and you shouldn't be out here—what did the doctor call it? 'Lurking?'" Blue lowered his dark eyebrows in what could have been a frown, except that the corners of his mouth twitched in a little smile.

"Sorry," Jack muttered.

"Anyway, I need you to do me a favor," Blue said.

"Sure!" Jack exclaimed, glad that Blue didn't seem angry. "What can I do for you?"

Motioning Jack to walk down the hall away from Heather's room, Blue explained, "There's a boy who's been living at our house for a few days because he needs a place to stay. This boy's mother is a real good friend of my wife, and the mother was in a bad car wreck last week. Really serious. She's right here in this hospital, room 234. I need you to go to that room and tell Merle we'll be ready to leave in a little while, and I want him to meet us in the parking lot so I can drive him back to our house."

"Merle?" Jack asked. "Is that his first name?"

"Yeah, Merle. His last name's Chapman. His mother is Arlene Chapman. She's the patient in room 234, in the next wing over that way." Blue pointed. "Tell Merle I'll call his mother's room when we're ready to go. You stay there with him 'til the call comes."

"OK." That didn't sound like anything Jack would really want to do, but at least he wasn't getting slammed for eavesdropping. Blue turned to go back into Heather's room, this time closing the door tightly behind him.

CHAPTER THREE

A rrows at the end of the hall pointed the way to rooms 220 through 240. Jack didn't hurry. He was not anxious to go inside a hospital room where he'd have to look at a woman who'd been badly hurt in a car wreck. Heather McDonald's leg, bandaged from hip to knee, had been disturbing enough to see. This Merle guy's mother might look a whole lot worse.

But as he came close to room 234, Jack heard laughter and the chatter of female voices. For a minute he wondered if it was the right room. When he peered inside, he saw a boy standing at the foot of a hospital bed, holding a guitar straight up by the neck as it rested on the mattress. Sitting next to the guitar was a woman wearing a pale blue hospital gown dotted with darker blue flowers. The boy must be Merle, and the woman his mother. They might have looked alike if her face hadn't been covered by two strips of tape that stretched from her forehead to her cheeks, crossing over her nose in a big *X*.

"Don't make Arlene laugh," a woman in a nurse's aide uniform warned two other women. "She has a tube in her chest because of that punctured lung. Laughing hurts her. I mean, it doesn't do any damage, it's just painful."

"Ooops! Sorry!" exclaimed one of the women, who was actually somewhere in between a woman and girl. Thin and pretty, she wore a nametag pinned to a green sweater, but she didn't look like a nurse's aide. Next to her, an older woman in a blue work shirt and jeans stood facing away from Jack so he couldn't see her too well, but in her back pocket he noticed a pair of garden clippers.

"Uh…are you Merle?" Jack asked from the doorway.

"Yeah," Merle answered. "Who are you?"

"My name's Jack Landon. My mom is helping Ranger Firekiller investigate today's bear attack. He said to tell you he'll be leaving here pretty soon."

Merle started to speak, but his mother held out her hand and said, "Pleased to meet you, Jack. I'm Arlene, and that cute young thing there is Corinn, and the hard-workin' lady reachin' out to shake your other hand is Bess. Poor Bess's been havin' to work twice as hard now that I'm not taggin' around after her in Dollywood, like I usually do. Bess and Corinn came here to see if I was makin' any progress. Wasn't that nice?"

Arlene Chapman looked like she needed a lot more progress. Beneath the X-shaped bandage, her nose was black and blue. Her eyes looked even more bruised, and she panted a little when she spoke, probably from that collapsed lung with the tube in it.

Speaking up again, Merle told Jack. "I gotta be at my job in Gatlinburg by 5:30. Bess said she'd drive me there tonight, and my boss will drive me back to the Firekillers' house after work."

Bess, the woman wearing work clothes, spoke up, "But you gotta pay me back, Merle. For the ride, I mean."

"How, Bess?" he asked.

"Sing one more song before we go."

The nurse's aide had left the room, but she poked her head around the door again, saying, "I heard that! Is Merle going to sing again? Sing loud, Merle, so I can hear you from the nurse's station."

So Merle was a singer? He didn't look more than a year older than Jack. In fact, he looked something *like* Jack, only taller and stockier, with hair a little redder than Jack's blond color and eyes more gray than blue.

Plucking a few strings on his guitar, Merle announced, "I'll sing this one 'cause Mom likes it best." He waited just a moment, strummed a chord, then began to sing:

> *Downtown by the neon lights*
> *Where trouble runs and the young men fight*
> *There's a woman singin' slow*
> *Her voice is rough and low*
> *And when she steps to the microphone*
> *The songs she sings are all her own....*

Jack straightened in surprise. Merle was good! Really good! The song went on:

> *Now I might seem as far apart*
> *From Mona's world as day from dark*
> *But Mona sings her soul to me*
> *And all her songs, they set me free*
> *She makes me feel I'm not alone*
> *She sings for me as if I was her own.*

The women in the room applauded, yelling *"yay"* and *"whoo hoo."* By then Jack wasn't just surprised, he'd zoomed all the way to astonished! Merle was as good as any singer Jack had ever heard on the radio or on television.

"That's my favorite of all the songs Merle ever wrote," his mother was saying, as she smiled and nodded her head.

"You wrote that song? Yourself?" Jack stammered.

"Yes, he did," Arlene answered proudly. "You know, we named Merle after the country singer Merle Haggard. When he grows up, Merle's gonna be just as famous as Merle Haggard."

Who was Merle Haggard? Jack had never heard of him.

Bess asked, "You used to sing, too, Arlene, didn't you? Back a ways?"

"Well, yes, I did. When Merle's daddy was alive, we

NIGHT OF THE BLACK BEAR

sang together. We wanted to be another Johnny Cash and June Carter, can you imagine?" She laughed a little at that, then clutched her chest, saying, "Ooh, that hurts!"

Johnny Cash! Jack knew about Johnny Cash. "I worked on a Johnny Cash CD cover," he said.

For a few silent seconds, everyone stared at Jack in amazement. "You...you designed a Johnny Cash record cover? By yourself?" Merle asked.

"No! No, I mean...I never designed it for real. I just fool around with Photoshop. Like...I change pictures to make them look funny or scary. Then I post them to a blog."

"Oh." They all looked a little disappointed. "Well, let's see your Johnny Cash cover then," Corinn told him, pulling a small laptop from a briefcase near her feet. "I brought my computer today so we could go over Arlene's Dollywood hospital insurance plan. Here, I'll turn it on for you."

Jack wished he'd never mentioned Photoshopping. He felt really stupid as he moved over to the computer Corinn set up on the bedside stand. Taking a deep breath, he signed into the blog and pulled up the picture he'd posted.

There it was, a CD cover of country music superstar Johnny Cash with his famous black shirt and pants all covered with one-dollar bills Jack had pasted on him digitally. "I call it 'Cash on Cash,'" he said weakly.

Their reaction was a big surprise. Corinn, Bess, and Merle burst out laughing, and Arlene cried, "Oooh, let me see! That is so funny. 'Cash on Cash!'"

Bess told Jack, "If you did a cover of Merle Haggard, you could make him look haggard—you know, all old and wore out."

The others laughed even louder when Arlene said, "How 'bout Martina McBride in a weddin' gown?"

Corinn, the younger one, must have sensed that Jack didn't recognize those names. In a quieter voice she told him, "You're not from around here, are you, Jack? This is the home of Dollywood and Nashville, the country music capital of the whole wide world. Every one of us Tennesseans grew up listening to country singers and country music, 'cause it's all about us and who we are."

Before Jack had a chance to answer, the phone rang, and Bess picked it up since Arlene couldn't reach it. "It's Blue," she announced. "He says to come right down to the parking lot."

After Jack said good-bye to the women, Merle told him, "I'll walk you down the hall so I can tell Blue I already got a ride to Gatlinburg." As they ambled slowly, Merle exclaimed, "You're a real artist, Jack, to do stuff like that. How did you learn it? I wish I could do that, but I don't have a computer at home."

No computer? Jack didn't know what he'd do without his own computer—it connected him to the world. He took a closer look at Merle, noticing that he wore a sweatshirt and stained pants that might have come out of a thrift shop. His shoes were pretty worn, with the rubber on the side of the soles discolored and cracked.

Merle's mother had mentioned that his father was dead. "Your mother works at Dollywood?" Jack asked. "What does she do there?"

"She's a groundskeeper. She goes around trimmin' bushes and sprayin' bugs and stuff. She won't be able to work for a while, though. That punctured lung will take a long time to get better. That's why I'm lucky I got this job."

Lucky? It sounded like the only luck they had was bad luck. Just as Jack was about to ask Merle what kind of job he had, he noticed Yonah coming toward them down the hall, walking fast.

"Uh-oh," Merle said, just before Yonah caught up to them. "Here comes Yonah the fire-spitter."

"You mean Firekiller," Jack corrected him.

"Wait 'til you know him better," Merle said.

"What's taking you so long?" Yonah demanded. "My dad's been waiting in the parking lot."

"Tell your dad he doesn't have to wait for me. I got another ride to Gatlinburg. So back off, man," Merle told Yonah. To Jack, he said, "It was good meeting you. Real good. Your work is cooler than frost. I'd like to see more of it."

With that, he was gone, and Jack had to follow Yonah. "Waste of time...coming after Merle," Yonah was muttering, hotly.

Jack remembered that Yonah's mother and Arlene Chapman were supposed to be good friends. Yet Yonah hadn't even stopped in the room to ask Arlene how she was feeling. What a jerk! Why did Ashley think Yonah was so great? Jack was glad they didn't have to ride home with him.

On the way back to their hotel in Gatlinburg, Jack talked excitedly to his parents about Arlene and Merle and Merle's great singing until Ashley cried, "All right! We get it! He can sing. But Yonah doesn't like him."

"How'd you know that?" Jack asked her.

"I saw Yonah's face when he told his dad that Merle wouldn't be coming home with them. His dad told him to cool it, that it didn't matter."

"Yeah, well if I had to hold an election between Merle and Yonah, I know who'd win."

"Enough!" Olivia called back. "Please be quiet for a while. I have a lot of thinking to do." After a few minutes she said, "We need to watch the evening news to find out what that Greta will say about the bear attacks and the park. I don't want to miss any of it, so I think we should have dinner in our rooms instead of going out to a restaurant."

The Landons were staying in two connecting rooms at the Gatlinburg Lodge, which meant Jack had to share with his sister. Ashley didn't like that at all, and Jack liked it even less because Ashley was always locking herself in the bathroom so she could mess with her hair. If Jack pounded on the door to make her come out, his mother or father would yell at him to stop.

That evening, while Olivia was pushing buttons on the remote to make sure she could find Greta's TV channel, Steven brought all of them Philly cheese steaks and milk shakes he'd ordered from a fast-food place across the street.

"Here it comes," Olivia announced just as Jack was licking his fingers after his meal. "The local news is on."

And there they were. All four Landons on the television screen, right there in room 112 of the Gatlinburg Lodge.

"Look at me!" Ashley cried happily. "I've never been on TV before." But it lasted only a few seconds before Greta's face and voice dominated the program.

"Good evening, Channel 12 viewers. This afternoon our news team got right on top of a breaking story in Great Smoky Mountains National Park. Sixteen-year-old Heather McDonald from Morganton, North Carolina, was mauled by a bear on the grounds of the old Methodist church in Cades Cove."

On the screen was a photo of Heather, not all band-aged the way they'd seen her in the hospital, but smiling and pretty, probably from her high school yearbook.

"Heather McDonald suffered a severe trauma to her

thigh," Greta continued, "where a large portion of her flesh was ripped away from the bone by a black bear. The bear has not yet been identified or caught. This marks the third bear attack in three weeks, two inside the park, and one at the Gatlinburg garbage dump."

"Oh, boy," Steven breathed.

"Oh, yuck!" Ashley cried, as the screen filled with images of other attack victims whose stories Greta told in full detail. The camera zoomed in on a woman's bloodied arm, and then shifted to a man holding up his ripped shirt as he pointed to four deep scratch marks that sliced his chest from the collar bone to his belt.

Jack yelled, "Look! There's Mom!"

"Olivia Landon," Greta's voice-over told the viewers, "is a wildlife veterinarian from Jackson Hole, Wyoming, who came to the park to confer with other wildlife experts. But Dr. Landon refused to make any statements about a possible reason for this sudden rash of bear attacks in our area."

Next came the scene just as Jack remembered it— Greta following Olivia and asking, "Dr. Landon, do you think it's in the public's best interest to shut down Great Smoky Mountains National Park?" And Olivia, trying to escape that dangling microphone as she edged toward the car, answering, "Ranger Firekiller has already told you that you'll need to discuss that with the park superintendent." The picture zoomed to the Landons' car driving out of the parking lot, with Jack's and Ashley's heads barely visible in the back seat.

Then came the bombshell. "Channel 12 has learned," Greta said now, "that Dr. Olivia Landon is an expert on elks. Not bears, but elks. This reporter wonders why, when visitors may be in real danger from bears at Great Smoky Mountains National Park, Dr. Landon is the person who's investigating the bear attacks. After all, so far we haven't been attacked by any elks."

"What! What did she just say?" Olivia jumped up from her chair, her dark eyes blazing with anger.

"Take it easy," Steven tried to calm her. "Don't worry about it, honey. She's just some news person who hasn't heard about all the animal mysteries you've solved at other parks."

Olivia wasn't about to calm down. It wasn't often that she lost her temper, but when she did, color rose to her cheeks and her five-foot-four height seemed to suddenly stretch by inches.

"I got called to this park to confer with Kip about elk rehabilitation," she stormed. "We didn't know there was going to be a bear attack...." Pointing to Greta on the TV, Olivia vowed, "You just wait! I'll solve this mystery so fast and so completely that Channel 12 will have to apologize—on the air!"

Jack couldn't help grinning. "Way to go, Mom," he told her.

"I'm starting right now!" Olivia resolved. "Steven, bring plenty of film tomorrow. Be sure to pack your digital camera, too. We're going to scour each of the attack locations, and you can photograph them inch by inch. I'll call Kip and Blue. Kids, why don't you get ready for bed now. We'll need to get an early start."

"Are you going to bed, too?" Ashley asked.

"No. I'll be reading every line of every report about black bears in Great Smoky Mountains National Park."

CHAPTER FOUR

Saturday, early, the four Landons headed out in their car. Olivia didn't look as if she'd been up late reading reports. She looked full of energy and ready to take charge.

"The plan is to begin with the elk," she announced, "since, as Greta so pointedly mentioned, that's my area of expertise."

"I don't want to sound like I'm on Greta's team, Mom," Jack told her, "but what exactly are you looking for with the elk?"

"The possibility that some of the elk might have been infected with the brucellosis bacteria—we know that disease causes problems with elk and cattle in Wyoming. And if a bear were to eat a sick elk calf, could the elk's disease organisms cause a strange reaction in the bear? There are so many unknowns! Your dad will photograph the whole area for bear tracks and scat or any other evidence."

Jack wished he could go along and take pictures with his own digital camera, but other plans had been made for the two Landon kids.

"It's real nice of Blue's wife to let you stay at their house this morning," Steven commented.

Ashley nodded as though she totally agreed, but Jack wasn't too sure. "Will Merle be there?" he asked.

"I imagine so." Steven was following the signs to Buckhorn Road, where the Firekillers lived at the top of a hill on the edge of Gatlinburg. He added, "Blue said Merle's staying with them at least until his mother gets out of the hospital. Maybe longer, if Arlene isn't strong enough to take care of herself."

"Poor Merle. Living in the same house with Yonah," Jack muttered.

"Poor Yonah!" Ashley exclaimed. "Living in the same house with Merle."

"What do *you* know! You've never even met Merle."

Their mother turned to tell them, "You kids be polite to Mrs. Firekiller, and friendly to both Merle and Yonah. And quit arguing!"

Neither Jack nor Ashley answered, but when their mother turned around, they made faces at each other.

"Looks like it's going to be a good day to take pictures," Steven was saying. "Just a little bit of mist, but that will burn off in an hour or so. Do you have your camera, Jack?"

"Uh-huh." He patted the pocket of his zip-up fleece vest. That was the best thing about a small digital camera—it was easy to carry. His father didn't like digital as much. Steven claimed that real film still turned out the best, clearest, most detailed pictures. But Jack loved his palm-size digital camera because he could upload his shots onto a computer, and then create funny pictures like Cash on Cash. Or grotesque ones like Ashley with a long nose and fangs dripping blood.

The Firekiller house turned out to be small, but it had a wide fenced-in backyard inhabited by a wildly enthusiastic golden retriever that nearly knocked Jack over when she jumped up to greet him.

"Down, Lola. Down!" Yonah commanded.

Jack and Ashley had already said their hellos to Mrs. Firekiller and were outside looking for Merle—that is, Jack looked for Merle. Yonah was showing Ashley four Cherokee masks he'd carved. A wolf, a bird, a deer, and one face mask painted all blue.

"For the Blue Clan," Yonah explained, "where my dad gets his name."

"You made all those yourself, Yonah? They're beautiful," gushed Ashley.

"This other one is gonna be my favorite when I finish it." Yonah lifted a half-carved gourd, saying, "I still have to glue on some buffalo hair, plus rawhide and a wild turkey feather. It's a booger mask."

"Booger? Did you say booger?" Ashley giggled and wrinkled her nose.

"Yeah. Cherokee men do the booger dance to make

fun of their enemies." Yonah held the unfinished gourd close to his face with one hand, slapped his chest with the other and yelled, *"Woo hoo!* I'll grind you to dust, Paleface."

Just then Merle came out of a shed at the back of the yard, pushing a red bicycle that rattled a bit as it rolled across the grass.

"I think I got it fixed," he said. "The chain was loose. Hi, Jack. Is Yonah showing you his boogers? Check his nose—he's got a lot of boogers."

"He's showing us his fantastic artwork," Ashley answered, without smiling. "You must be Merle."

"Hey, wait here, I want you to see what else I made," Yonah told them. With Lola tearing around in circles and nearly tripping him, Yonah ran across the yard to the shed Merle had just left. In half a minute he came out carrying four poles that looked like lacrosse sticks, but they were shorter, the heads were narrower, and they were strung with sinews instead of mesh. Tossing a ball into the air and catching it, he asked, "You guys want to play? I can take on both Jack and Merle."

"You have four sticks there," Ashley told him. "Let me play, too."

"Hey, I don't think…," Merle began.

Yonah broke in with, "She can if she wants. Cherokee girls have their own stickball teams, and they're good at the game. I bet Ashley will play great."

So this was stickball, not lacrosse. Yonah's backyard was plenty big enough for any kind of sport, but first Jack needed to find out the rules of the game.

"You know lacrosse?" Merle asked him. "Stickball's just another name for lacrosse."

"No way!" Yonah scoffed. "Us Redmen played stickball centuries before you rednecks had lacrosse." The ball he held was not made of rubber, but covered with deerskin. "In a real game, we're supposed to take off our shirts—" Yonah began.

"You definitely do not mean me," Ashley announced.

Laughing, Yonah answered, "Definitely not you, Ashley. I meant the guys. Indian stickball is played by guys with bare chests and bare feet. But we'll keep our shirts on because it's chilly this morning, and we'll keep our shoes on because Lola uses this yard for her bathroom, and...uh...you get the picture."

Jack pulled off his fleece vest, anyway—he felt warm enough in his long-sleeve polo shirt. Merle had on a faded T-shirt with a Detroit Tigers logo. Jack figured he and Merle were supposed to team up against Yonah and Ashley. The blonds against the dark-hairs.

After Yonah tied Lola to a porch post, he slapped his chest and yelled, "WOOOO HOOOOO. Let's play!" Scooping up the ball, he flung it against a tree at the end of the yard before Jack even knew that was the goal. Jack found out fast that in this game there was no net, and if the ball hit certain tree branches, that was a score. No out-of-bounds, no offsides, no boundary lines of any kind, no time-outs, no halftime, no fouls, no free throws. And, "No tackling!" Merle yelled. "There's a girl playing!"

And did she ever play! Ashley's long, dark hair swirled around her shoulders as she picked up the deerskin ball with her webbed stick and ran toward the goal, dodging both Merle and Jack. "How many goals do we need to win?" she shouted to Yonah.

"Eight!"

They'd better get serious then, Jack thought. "Hey! I saw her carrying that ball in her hand," he yelled.

"That's allowed," Yonah shot back. "In Cherokee stickball, after you pick up the ball with your stick, you can grab it in your hand and run."

"I know the rules," Merle muttered, "and I'm not gonna get beaten by a girl. Even if she is cute."

Jack turned to stare at Merle. He didn't see the ball coming until it hit him in the knee.

"War wound, Paleface!" Yonah yelled.

"I'm OK!" Jack yelled back, and to Merle, "You're right. We gotta win this."

The game grew intense. Yonah's sweaty hair kept falling in his eyes, making Jack glad his own hair was cut short. Ashley's shirt got damp under the arms, and the guys' faces shone with sweat, especially Merle's. Since Merle was stockier, he had more weight to move around, and that made him sweat more, Jack guessed. It was a simple game with hardly any rules—back and forth in the yard, picking up the deerskin ball with the sticks, flinging it or running with it. The score stayed pretty even: four goals for Jack, three for Merle, three for Ashley, four for Yonah.

And then Yonah scored the eighth goal. "We won!" he hollered, throwing his stick into the air and smacking hands with Ashley, who flung back her hair and did a little victory dance.

After Yonah untied Lola, Ashley laughed and started her dance again, this time with the exuberant dog. The three of them jumped around in a circle, with Ashley and Yonah patting their mouths and shouting *"woo woo woo woo"* in a war chant, while Lola barked.

Mrs. Firekiller came out onto the back porch then, carrying a tray. A pretty woman with skin paler than Blue's or Yonah's, she had the same thick black hair.

"I watched you through the window. Great game!" she told them. "You're probably thirsty and hungry after all that exercise." She set the tray on the edge of the back steps and said, "Here's bottled water, lemonade, and some towels to wipe off your sweat. Plus my special fry bread; you can put peanut butter and jelly on it if you want to." As the kids gathered around Mrs. Firekiller— she told them to call her Lily—she sat on the steps and poured lemonade for them.

Jack had tasted fry bread many times before—after all, Wyoming was Indian country—but Mrs. Firekiller's was especially good.

"Let's go for a bike ride," Merle urged, before Jack had a chance to finish eating. "Is it OK if Ashley uses your bike, Lily? And Jack can take Blue's?"

"Sure, that's fine," she agreed. "Take these water bottles with you, and I'll get you some trail mix. But watch out for bears." She hesitated. "You know, it seems strange to have to warn you about bears. Each year millions of people come to this park hoping to see black bears, and most of them are disappointed because the bears stay hidden. And now, suddenly, people are getting attacked. I wish we knew what's going on."

Merle didn't wait for Lily to finish talking. He started wheeling the bikes out of the shed, one at a time.

Thanking Lily for everything, Jack and Ashley followed Merle and Yonah onto the street, heading north. Within a mile they'd crossed the boundary into Great Smoky Mountains National Park. Jack got the feeling that this bike ride was just one more competition between Merle and Yonah, with Merle trying to make up for the stickball defeat. The bikes were new, sleek, fast, and probably expensive, all except Merle's. His bike still rattled. Jack and Ashley had to pump hard to keep up with the other two. First, Merle was in the lead, then Yonah. Once Merle came close to clipping Yonah's front wheel when he cut in front of him.

"Slow *down*," Ashley yelled. "I want to enjoy the scenery. Look at all these butterflies—I've never seen so many butterflies in one place in my life!"

The butterflies really were amazing, sailing and swooping high and then low enough to almost brush the kids' shoulders as they biked. Pale gray ones with spotted wings; beautiful black ones with white dots that looked like eyes edging the wings; others of pale yellow rimmed with black, blue, and orange; or pure yellow, or bright orange, and even plain light brown ones that flitted around their spectacular cousins as though they weren't ashamed to look ordinary.

"I feel like I'm in a fantasy world," Ashley sang out.

Merle glanced back at Jack and grinned. Since Merle didn't have any sisters, he wasn't used to girly outbursts, Jack guessed. Suddenly, Merle cut crosswise in front of Yonah, coming to a stop with a skid and making Yonah and everyone else nearly run into him.

"What the—what are you doing?" Yonah yelled.

"I want you to pull your bikes through this opening into the trees," Merle told everyone. We're gonna leave them over there so I can show you guys something."

"Are you sure it's all right to park the bikes here?" Jack asked, as they followed Merle through foliage that had just begun to leaf out in earnest. "I mean, this bike belongs to Yonah's father. It'd be real bad if someone stole it."

"No one'll steal it," Merle promised.

"Like you know that," Yonah argued.

"Nobody's out here but us and the bears."

"That's a stupid thing to say," Yonah told Merle. "You'll scare Ashley."

Maybe Ashley was getting used to the bickering, because she ignored it, reaching out to the butterflies. A dark blue one landed on her outstretched fingers, raising and lowering its wings and waving its antennae.

"If you guys want to go see whatever this *thing* is that Merle's so hot to show you, I'll wait here," Yonah growled.

"Oh, come with us," Ashley told him, and took his hand. Surprisingly, Yonah followed her. Wow! Jack thought, how'd she make that happen?

They were on a barely visible trail, winding through newly leafed trees that stood so tall and so close together they made Jack feel dwarfed. The trees grew thicker, and the leaves rustled—from wind? Or was there some critter back there in the woods? Maybe Merle hadn't been joking. Maybe there *were* bears around here. Close by!

Jack saw Ashley's eyes widen, and he knew she was thinking the same thing. That happened often, that they shared thoughts without speaking them. He remembered last night's evening news, showing the bloody wounds of the bear victims on TV. And he remembered the blood on the ground in the cemetery. But he didn't want to say anything, because he didn't want Merle and Yonah to think he was a wimp. Yonah, especially. Those two guys were forging ahead through the trees as if they were someplace safe, not inside the boundaries of Great Smoky Mountains National Park, where bears had been eating people lately.

After about a tenth of a mile, they came to a small clearing. Merle stopped, held out an arm, and said, "This is what I wanted you to see. Look over there."

At first Jack thought it was just a pile of rocks Merle pointed to, then he realized it was stones mortared together. "That's what's left of the chimney," Merle said. "This used to be the Chapman family farm. My great-granddaddy built a house here, cleared the land, and raised kids and cows and corn."

"It's mostly trees now," Jack observed.

"Yeah, but not back then. My granddaddy grew up here. When he was a kid, he'd hoe corn for 12 hours a day and get paid just 25 cents, he told me. And when he got bigger he carried hundred-pound sacks of sugar, one on each shoulder, for the moonshiners."

Ashley looked puzzled. "What are 'moonshiners?'"

It was Yonah who answered, "They're the lawbreakers who made their own whiskey in illegal stills, until they were arrested by federal agents."

"Nah, they hardly ever got arrested," Merle said. "And they weren't criminals. Even during Prohibition, every family in these mountains grew corn and made moonshine from it, either to drink or to sell. City folks were always willin' and waitin' to buy 'shine."

Merle seemed to be admitting that his kinfolk were lawbreakers. "If they had farms here," Jack asked, "why did they leave?"

Yonah was the one who answered. "Look around you. You're now standing in Great Smoky Mountains National Park. How do you think it got here?"

Merle nodded. "The landowners got kicked out so the U.S. government could turn all this scenery into a national park. It was back in the Depression, and my family had to sell the land dirt cheap. Great-granddaddy put the money into a bank, and then the bank went bust. So there he was—no money, nine kids, and no job 'cause all the other people were looking for jobs, too."

Yonah's face screwed up as he mocked, "Oh, *boo hoo hoo!* So your kinfolk got kicked off the land. Hey, Jack, want to know how Merle's kinfolk got the land in the first place? They stole it from the Cherokee Nation! The Cherokees happened to be here first, and they got run right off this land, with guns pointed at their backs!"

Now it was Yonah who threw out his arms. "About a thousand years ago the Cherokee people settled all the land from the Ohio River to South Carolina. They were doing just great…'til the Europeans came."

The way he said "Europeans" made Jack uncomfortable. After all, his own ancestors came from Europe.

"This was our sacred ancestral home," Yonah went on. "And listen to this, Ashley—the Cherokee men treated their women as equals. Yeah! And that was long before white men did that."

"So what happened?" Ashley asked softly. "What happened to all of them?"

"The U.S. President Andrew Jackson sent American soldiers to force 14,000 Cherokee from the land around here. And those tribes didn't get paid in dollars—they got paid *nothing*. The soldiers marched them all the way to Oklahoma. In winter!" Yonah was growing agitated. "Thousands of Cherokee people died along the way, mostly women and kids."

Even Merle was silent now, staring at the ground. Jack wondered which of the two guys had won the argument. Not a good kind of argument—a "my folks were treated worse then yours" contest. No real winners.

"Hey, check over there," Ashley said, walking a little way ahead. "It's like there's an old pot or something behind those trees. Maybe it got left behind when everyone had to move away."

That Ashley—she had sharp eyes! Jack wouldn't have noticed the slight gleam of copper barely visible through the brush; in fact, it looked as though brush had been deliberately piled on top of it.

"Uh-oh," Merle muttered.

"I know what it is," Yonah yelled. "It's a still. Where

Merle's great-grandfather made his moonshine." He rushed forward and began to pull away the brush, revealing a large round copper pot sealed with a lid. A stovepipe rose out of the lid, then narrowed and curved downward to connect to a smaller copper tub.

Merle looked slightly embarrassed, but he smiled. "Yup, that's what it is. A still. Good ol' great-granddaddy."

Close to the still were two wooden barrels, one standing, one lying on its side. As Jack circled around to get a better view, he asked, "What's this stuff that spilled out of the barrel onto the ground?"

"That's mash," Yonah answered. "Corn mash. Moonshiners grind up the corn, mix it with yeast and other stuff, then let it ferment and turn into moonshine. But, oh man, this spilled mash here isn't anything Merle's great-granddaddy left behind. It looks pretty fresh."

"No it doesn't," Merle said. "It's not all that fresh because some of the corn kernels are sprouting, see that? This spilled mash has been here a while. Well, OK, maybe not that long, but maybe a couple of weeks."

"So who's up here making moonshine? Some of your redneck cousins, Merle?" Yonah taunted him.

Merle shrugged. "They've been known to do that."

"You know what I think?" Ashley suddenly cried out. "I bet some bears came, knocked over this barrel, and ate some of the mash. It made them drunk, and they got mean. That's why the bear attacked Heather. He was drunk!"

"No way," Merle said. "That's not the reason."

"What do you know about it?" Yonah demanded. "I think it's a pretty good theory, Ashley. It really could explain why two bear attacks happened in the park in the past ten days. You don't know anything about bears, Merle, so shut up."

Merle not only shut up, he clamped his lips tight, lowered his eyes, and sauntered away. That was unusual. It was the first time he'd let Yonah slam him without pushing back.

Pulling his camera from his vest pocket, Jack said, "I'll take pictures of this and show them to my mom and Kip and Blue. If they think maybe bears did get into the mash, they can come out here to investigate. Then they can check for bear hair and claw marks and stuff." He looked up and called, "Hey, where are you going, Merle?"

"To make sure the bikes are OK," Merle answered. "I'll meet you back there."

"Oh, OK. Later." Jack began to take pictures. Just as his dad had taught him, he shot from every angle, circling the copper kettles and the spilled mash. The light was good, he avoided shadows, and after a dozen shots he could tell he'd taken some good ones.

When he finished, he, Yonah, and Ashley went back to get the bikes. Merle was gone.

CHAPTER FIVE

"Where'd he go?" Jack asked Yonah, bewildered.

"Don't worry—Merle knows his way around."

Their bikes were still leaning up against the trees, undisturbed. Jack was tempted to say, See, Yonah, no one stole them, just like Merle said, but he thought he'd better not.

After the three of them biked back to the Firekillers', Jack found Merle in the shed.

Bent over his red bike, he greeted Jack with, "Can't get this chain to stop rattling. I'm tryin' to tighten it."

"Can I help?" Jack volunteered, but Merle just shook his head.

It was an old bike, from the looks of it. By contrast, the bike Jack had ridden into the park, the one that belonged to Blue Firekiller, was a sleek new mountain bike.

"Why'd you leave us back there?" Jack asked him.

"I just get tired of Yonah comin' down on me all the time. Yeah, I know he's smart—he takes college-level calculus and advanced history of western civilization and he's only a junior. But he acts like me and my family are a bunch of dumb rednecks." Merle gave a yank to a wrench handle, tightening a bolt.

Before Jack could answer, Merle went on, "I come from hard-workin' people. My daddy died in a logging accident when I was four, and my mom tries real hard to keep her and me goin'. Yonah's mom and dad both have jobs, so they can pay for a nice house like this, and they can buy fancy bikes and—" He bounced his own bike on the floor of the shed, shaking his head when the chain still rattled.

Turning to stare straight into Jack's eyes, Merle said, "For now, I'll take any job I can get. But someday I'm gonna be a famous singer and buy my mom a bigger house than this one, even, and a car. We don't have a car now that it got wrecked...." He stopped then, looking a bit embarrassed. "Hey, why am I whinin' to you like this, Jack? Blah, blah, blah. Just tell me to shut up."

"No, it's OK. Where do you work, Merle?"

Merle seemed to hesitate before he answered, "The Sunset Grill in Gatlinburg. I'm a busboy. I better get my stuff together now so I won't be late. Don't wanna lose this job. I just got it a week ago."

Not long afterward, while Jack was watching Ashley and Yonah play Sudoku on a computer, he glanced through a window and noticed Merle riding away on his bike. His guitar case was strapped to his back. That's odd, Jack thought—why would he take his guitar to a busboy job? He didn't bother to ask Yonah, because Yonah would just answer with some negative jab at Merle. And he didn't ask Lily Firekiller, who came into the room a few minutes later.

"Kids, your parents just called. They want you to meet them in Gatlinburg. You, too, Yonah, because your dad's there. I'll drop off the three of you, and then I'll go on to the hospital to see if Arlene needs anything."

In the car, Ashley sat in the backseat with Yonah. They continued their Sudoku games, but this time in a magazine. The distance from the Firekillers' house to Gatlinburg was a little more than six miles. Six miles in a car was nothing, but it would be a pretty long bike ride for Merle.

Lily dropped them off at a building with an over-hanging sign small enough that they might have missed it—The Digital Oasis. Inside, Steven was eager to point out some of the equipment to Jack.

"Five workstations, all dual-platform. They're total powerhouses! High-end software, top of the line graphics-intensive," Steven marveled.

"I thought you didn't like digital photos, Dad," Jack reminded him.

"Normally not. But today I used a digital camera when I photographed the elk herd. Digital is faster, and we're in a big hurry," Steven explained, "so Blue told us about this lab."

Glancing at the wall clock, Olivia said, "It's almost six. We've already downloaded a lot of our pictures, so why don't we take a break and go to dinner, guys?"

"Yeah. We could go to that Sunset Grill where Merle works," Jack suggested.

"Let's just order pizza, and we'll eat it here," Steven answered. "I don't want to lose any time with these elk photos. This graphics-intensive software lets me examine each image almost pixel by pixel. We haven't found any evidence yet, but there's still a good chance we'll notice clues we missed out in the field."

Turning to Blue, Olivia asked, "OK with you if we get pizza delivered for us? The kids can eat out—there's nothing for them to do here, and they'll just get bored." Handing two $20s to Jack, she told him, "This should be more than enough for the place you mentioned. Yonah will know where it is."

"Uh-huh," Yonah nodded, with a twist of the lips Jack couldn't interpret.

They walked along the sidewalks of the busy town of Gatlinburg, where side-by-side tourist attractions grabbed attention even more than in Pigeon Forge. Ahead, in the distance, Jack saw the tree-covered elevations that Tennesseans called mountains. Folks around here ought to see what real mountains look like, he thought. From his bedroom window in Jackson Hole, Wyoming, Jack could look out at snow-covered peaks that reached nearly

14,000 feet, more than twice as high as the Smokies. Still, it was nice to see all those trees. Wyoming mountains were bare at the topmost peaks.

"There it is," Ashley announced. "The Sunset Grill."

It was an ordinary looking restaurant, Jack thought, and not too full of customers. As they entered, a hostess came up to them and asked, "Would you rather have a table or a booth?"

"Booth," Yonah replied. He'd hardly spoken at all during the walk to the restaurant, maybe because Ashley had kept up her nonstop chatter.

"Follow me," the hostess told them. She wore her hair in a long, blonde ponytail that swung from side to side as she walked ahead. After they were seated next to a window, Jack noticed that the top of her frilly apron was covered with pins and badges. One said "Elvis is Alive in Gatlinburg," another one said "I Got High in the Space Needle," another showed a fancy car with the words "Hollywood Star Cars Museum." There were lots more badges, and above them was her nametag—Caitlyn.

"What are you, a walking advertisement for Gatlinburg tourists?" Yonah asked Caitlyn.

"Why not?" she answered, smiling brightly at Yonah. She kept her eyes on Yonah as she handed out the menus and told him, "Andrew will be your server tonight, but if you need anything at all, just ask me! Remember, I'm Caitlyn."

She started to walk away when Jack stopped her with, "There's a guy named Merle Chapman who works here. He's a busboy. Will you please tell him we're here so we can say hi?"

Caitlyn stopped. Turning around, she answered, "There's no Merle here."

"Merle Chapman," Jack repeated. "Kind of husky, reddish blond hair. Maybe you haven't met him yet because he's new at this job."

"I know everyone who works here," Caitlyn said definitely. "No one's named Merle." As she left them then, after one more smile at Yonah, Jack wondered if he'd gotten the restaurant's name wrong. Ashley raised her eyebrows questioningly. Yonah looked totally *not* surprised.

"I'm almost positive Merle said Sunset Grill," Jack said a bit puzzled.

"Yeah. That's what Merle told me when he took off for this supposed-to-be job a few nights ago," Yonah nodded.

"Supposed to be? What does that mean?" Jack asked.

"It means Merle's a big fat liar. He doesn't work here. I never believed he did. Let's see, I think I'll have a double burger with fries. And a shake. What are you guys going to order?"

Ashley and Jack glanced uncertainly at each other, then looked down at their menus. Yonah seemed to be telling them, no more questions, not now.

When their meals arrived—Ashley got a plate of popcorn shrimp and Jack had a double burger like Yonah's—their talk sounded almost normal. Almost, but not quite. Puzzlement over Merle's lie, if it really was a lie, seemed to hang like a mist above the table, the way clouds of mist hang over the peaks of the Great Smoky Mountains.

Ashley, who never hesitated to speak what was on her mind, slowly stirred her lemonade with a straw as though this time, perhaps, it would be wise to be more careful with her words. But after a few moments she frowned, tossed her head, and came right out with it. "Why do you hate Merle?" she asked Yonah.

It seemed to catch him by surprise. He hesitated before he answered, "'Hate' is a strong word. I don't really hate him. I just don't want to be connected to him. Since we were little, he's been like a fly buzzing around me—always there, always a nuisance."

"Because your mothers are friends?" Ashley asked.

"Right. They're almost like sisters, especially after Merle's dad died. My mom kept helping out because things were so hard for Arlene Chapman." Yonah took a long drink of his milk shake, rubbed his forehead, and said, *"Whoo!* Brain freeze. I hate those. Do you ever get brain freeze?" After a pause he added, "Now Merle—he doesn't freeze my brain, he frosts my shorts. Ha!"

"Yeah, funny." Ashley laughed a little, halfheartedly. "But why, Yonah? You still didn't say why."

Looking through the window at the Gatlinburg street traffic, Yonah said, "Oh—I guess it goes a long way back. OK! Here's an example." He drummed his fingers on the table and began, "I'm a year and a half older than Merle, so my mom was always giving him my outgrown clothes and stuff. No problem there. But she'd let him have my toys, too. Sometimes I wasn't through with them. She'd say, 'You have lots to play with, Yonah, and Merle's mother can't afford to buy him things. You need to share.'"

"That sounds...nice of her," Jack murmured.

"Yeah? Well, I didn't care about balls and books and stuff, but one time, something happened that...." Yonah drew circles on damp sides of his glass as he continued, "There was this one thing I really loved. A Chief Cherokee action figure. It belonged to my dad when he was little, and it was still in the box, with a ton of accessories—bows and arrows, a quiver, a buffalo-horn headpiece, a war bonnet, lots of other stuff. I was real careful with it. Each time I took the Chief and the other things out of the box to play with, I put them back exactly where they belonged."

"So what happened?" Ashley asked.

"Merle wanted it. My Chief Cherokee." Yonah set the glass on the table, hard. "He grabbed the box from my hands, and he tore it. So, I punched him, and his lip bled and he howled and my mom came running. She yelled at me and gave Merle my Chief Cherokee. To keep!"

Jack could see how that would make a little kid mad. "How old were you?"

"I was seven. Merle was almost six."

"Really." Ashley curled her fingers over the edge of the table as she leaned forward. "And you're still mad at him over *that?* After all these years? He was only a little kid!"

"No, that's not the *only* thing." Yonah glared at his hamburger, then picked it up and said, "Forget what I told you. Let's eat and get out of here."

Jack knew his sister was turning all this over and over in her mind, carefully examining Yonah's words as she searched for the heart of his conflict with Merle. Finally, when she pushed away her empty plate, she said to Yonah, "There's more, isn't there? I guess that Chief Cherokee thing was what started you being mad at Merle, but no one stays mad for nine years about something like that. That's not the real story. There's something a lot bigger. Right?"

They were interrupted by the hostess, Caitlyn, who approached carrying the check on a little tray. Standing close to Yonah, she handed it to him.

"I'll take that," Jack told her as he reached for it. "Am I supposed to give the money to you?"

"No. Pay up front," she answered.

Yonah had begun to get up to follow Caitlyn, but Jack stopped him with, "Wait! I'd like you to answer

Ashley's question—that maybe there's something much bigger. Is there?"

Yonah settled back into the booth, peeling a couple of dollar bills out of his wallet to leave as a tip—Jack had forgotten he was supposed to tip the server. "Why? Why should I answer Ashley's question? What's it to you guys?"

"Because," Ashley began slowly, "if I believed you hate Merle because he took a favorite toy from you when you were little—or even worse, if I believed that you hate him because he's a white guy and you blame him because his ancestors took Cherokee lands long ago— then I'd think that was way harsh. That *you* were harsh. And I don't think you are."

Smoothing the dollar bills on the table top, Yonah murmured, "Thanks. For not thinking I'm harsh." He looked up, his dark eyes troubled, and said, "Things are really bad for Arlene right now. The insurance won't pay for all her hospital bills, her car was totaled, and she might not be able to work for a while." He licked his lip with the tip of his tongue, looked sideways, and then began again. "I think Merle's in trouble. He's doing some- thing that's wrong, and I think I know what it is, and it makes me crazy angry. But I'm not sure about it. If I tell anyone what I suspect, Merle could get slammed. That would hurt Arlene, and I don't want that to happen."

"It's about him not being a busboy, right?" Jack asked. "I was trying to figure out why he'd lie about that, and this is what I think. He brings his guitar, so he's probably out on the streets somewhere singing for quarters, and he's ashamed for people to know that."

"Huh?" Yonah muttered. "If that was true, I'd have heard about it. My friends would see him, and they'd tell me. *Merle* would tell me. That's not illegal."

Jack asked, "You think he's doing something *illegal?* Like what?"

Yonah didn't answer that directly. He just said, "You heard Merle today—about the moonshine? He doesn't worry about what's legal and what's not."

Slowly standing up, Ashley said, "You're way too suspicious, Yonah."

Yonah got up, too, and shrugged, saying, "Think what you want." Without waiting for them, he left the dining room and headed for the door. Jack stopped to pay the bill, then hurried to catch up with Yonah and Ashley.

As they walked back toward the digital lab, Jack glanced across the street where a small bus was parked. The sides of the bus had been painted with scenes of the park, or at least he figured that's what the pictures showed—tall mountains filled with mist, and black bears standing on their hind legs, bears running, climbing, holding fish in their mouths, even boxing each other. "Smokies Touring Service" was the name on the side of the bus. As Jack watched, a dozen people started boarding it.

At that moment Ashley tugged the sleeve of his sweatshirt to say, "Check over there. It's that Space Needle in the picture on Caitlyn's badge. Look how tall it is! I want to go to the top."

"It's got a virtual reality roller coaster," Yonah told them. "You should ask your folks to take you."

"I will!"

As soon as they opened the door to the digital lab they smelled the pizza. An open box with a few pieces left lay on the table, next to three paper cups for soft drinks.

"So far, we can't find a tie-in between the elk herd and the aggressive bear behavior," Olivia announced to the kids.

All over the room, elk photos appeared on tall flat screens. They were dazzling pictures—clear, bright, and intense in color—elk with rough coats and soft brown eyes, elk gracefully moving their large bodies on thin legs, an elk scratching behind an ear with a hind hoof. But there were no signs of disease. Jack stared at the images, wide-eyed, hoping that some day he'd be as good a photographer as his father.

Moments later the door flew open again, and this time Kip Delaney burst in, calling out, "Glad you're all still here. I just got back from the lab in Knoxville." Dangling from his hand was a sealed plastic bag containing a digital camera. "Heather and Mrs. McDonald have already left for North Carolina, but I told them I'd send Heather's camera by express mail as soon as we finished the tests."

"What tests?" Jack asked his mother.

"The bear had that camera in his mouth," Olivia explained. "We wanted to check the camera for bear saliva. If we can get gene identification from the saliva, we'll know when we've caught the right bear—if we *do* catch him."

"How'd it go, Kip?" Blue asked.

Kip shook his head, answering, "No go. Too many people had handled the camera—that Jordan guy, the paramedics, the nurses at the hospital—there wasn't enough bear spit left to get a good analysis."

Olivia looked disappointed until Kip announced, "However...the flash card is still here in the camera. We can look at the pictures Heather took before the mauling."

"Good job!" Right away Steven inserted the flash card into the card reader. The first pictures to come up on the screens showed a tombstone that read "Howard McDonald 1912–1983 Rest In Peace." The next picture showed a smaller tombstone: "Grace Neely McDonald 1916–1982 Returning To The Arms of Jesus."

Then the photos got exciting. Steven clicked to change the images about every two seconds, making them appear one right after another. It was almost like watching a movie.

The bear could be seen in the distance, standing up, arms dangling. In the next picture he'd come closer, his mouth slightly open to show those big canine teeth that had ripped flesh out of Heather's thigh. The following pictures showed him first raising then lowering his head. Next, he raised one paw as his shoulders shifted, almost as if he were dancing. With each picture he moved forward, his head lowered. In the last photos he stood up tall again, and as his face came closer and closer, Jack felt like those two black eyes were staring straight into his own!

"That crazy girl!" Blue exclaimed. "I can't believe she kept taking these pictures. In this final one the bear's no more than five feet in front of her!"

Steven added, "Yeah, right before the bear grabbed the camera."

"Ugh!" Ashley cried. "I wouldn't want a bear coming after me like that. I mean, he's *big!*"

A pause, then, "You're right, Ashley," Kip said. "He's way too big."

All of them turned toward Kip, unsure what he meant. But Olivia caught more meaning than the rest of them. Frowning, she said, "Go on, please, Kip."

His finger on the keyboard, Kip clicked back to the first picture. "This black bear is a male. Males average around 175 or 200 pounds—you probably thought they were bigger than that, Ashley, but that's their average weight. The weight changes through the different seasons of the year."

He faced them. "At this time of year in the park, the black bears have just recently come out of their winter dens." To Ashley, Jack, and Yonah, he added, "Maybe you kids know this, maybe you don't, but the reason bears spend winters in their dens is because each autumn, their source of food decreases or is eliminated altogether. So after most of the food is gone, they just go to sleep to conserve their energy. Nature has programmed them to sleep when there's nothing much left to eat."

"Right," Olivia agreed. "It's called denning."

"So here it is, now—early spring," Kip continued. "Once bears wake up, their systems are really undernourished, and they're looking for food. They've been living off their own body resources while they were in the dens, and their weight is a lot lower than when they first went into their dens. At this time of year—right now—there isn't a lot of high quality natural food around, so—" Kip picked up a pencil to point at the bear on the screen. "This bear should be a lot thinner than he looks here."

"Strange," Steven murmured.

"Yeah. Maybe. Or not," Yonah said softly.

CHAPTER SIX

It was Sunday morning, early. This time Olivia drove, and Steven turned around from the front seat to tell Jack and Ashley, "Lily Firekiller just called on my cell phone. After we drop you off at the Firekiller house, she's planning to take you to the Space Needle in Gatlinburg. Yonah told her you wanted to go there."

"Yay!" Ashley cried. "Mrs. Firekiller is the *nicest* lady!"

"Next to you, Mom," Jack said, figuring it never hurt to throw out a little compliment, especially since his mother hadn't been making many touchdowns in trying to solve the bear mystery. "Where will you and dad be this morning?"

"Searching for clues again," Olivia said. "We have some big questions we're trying to answer—why these bear attacks happened, and most important, will we need to close the park?"

Jack was silent for a moment before he asked, "What about that spilled mash at the still? I mean that moonshine mash I took the pictures of. If the bear got drunk from it, he could have turned mean."

Slowing the car to make a turn, Olivia answered, "Your pictures were good, Jack, but they didn't show any evidence of bear activity. Blue is going to the farm to check out the site today just in case, but we don't expect he'll find anything." Then, pulling into a driveway, she announced, "OK, here we are at the Firekillers'."

Lily came to the door to greet them, and told them that Yonah wouldn't be going to the Space Needle. "He's been there lots of times, and he's upstairs now studying for a calculus exam tomorrow. He says he'll see you later—I'm inviting all of you to Sunday dinner after Blue and Kip and you Landons finish your work."

"Thank you!" Olivia and Steven both exclaimed wholeheartedly. "It'll be great to have a real home-cooked dinner after all the take-out food we've been eating since we arrived," Olivia added.

Right then a thundering of footsteps on the stairs grew loud as Merle rushed into the room, shouting, "I finished all my homework!" Raising his right hand, he said, "I swear I did, Lily! Can I go to the Space Needle with you all?"

Homework! Jack and Ashley were supposed to keep up with their assignments for the three days of school they would miss, but Jack hadn't opened a single book. Oh, well, he would deal with that on the long flight home.

"So, can I go to the Space Needle with you all?" Merle was pleading.

"Sure," Lily answered. "Let's get moving. Even on Sundays the Space Needle opens at nine, and I'd like to get there before it's too crowded."

The drive to Gatlinburg from the Firekillers' house on that quiet Sunday morning took no more than 12 minutes, but to Jack it seemed longer, because he shared the back-seat with Merle. After listening to all of Yonah's suspicions about Merle the evening before, Jack couldn't fall into the easy, friendly kind of talk they'd had during the bike ride. He kept remembering how casually Merle had spoken about the moonshine still, as though breaking that particular law didn't matter. He mentally questioned why Merle would insist on biking to his job, with the guitar case strapped to his back. Was Yonah right? Was Merle involved in something illegal? Or was Yonah totally off base, making up false accusations just because he didn't like Merle?

Merle didn't seem to notice that Jack stayed quiet. He kept talking enthusiastically about Jack's Photoshopped pictures, like the one of the fish with Ashley's face. Jack had downloaded some of the silly ones onto Lily's computer yesterday, and Merle said he'd looked at them several times because they were so funny.

"You're a real digital artist, Jack," Merle told him now. "Someday, if I ever make a CD, you can design the jacket."

"Uh-huh," Jack answered, beginning to feel even more uncomfortable.

The entrance to the Space Needle looked pretty ordinary until Jack stood still and raised his eyes all the way up to the observation platform, towering 400 feet above them. Lily Firekiller bought tickets for herself and Merle; Jack and Ashley paid for their own with money their dad had given them earlier.

It was a fast elevator ride all the way to the platform at the top. Jack was glad he'd brought his camera because the view was really spectacular: the city of Gatlinburg beneath them, the tree-covered hills so close he didn't need to zoom the lens to feel right on top of them, the clouds skimming the mountaintops, and way over there was Great Smoky Mountains National Park.

"See any bears through your zoom lens?" Ashley teased, knowing that was impossible.

Jack swung around and snapped a quick picture of her; he'd Photoshop it grotesquely when they got home to Wyoming. He could feel Merle's impatience, though, because Merle kept urging Lily about going to the virtual roller coaster. That meant more tickets to buy. And they weren't cheap.

Two to a pod, the four of them climbed into VR roller coaster seats, with Lily and Ashley in one pod and Merle and Jack in another. Bars swung down to secure them. Jack figured that must mean the pods actually flipped, so the ride would have real movement as well as virtual imaging to give the sense of speed.

"Whoa!" he yelled, when the ride started. It moved, all right—upside down! He was loving it, but one part of his brain kept thinking how cool it would be to create realistic virtual-reality graphics like the ones spinning around his head inside the pod. Maybe that's what he'd do when he got out of college.

"Cool!" he yelled, when it stopped.

"Wait 'til I show you what's next!" Merle shouted.

The two of them raced down some stairs to an amusement area that had a laser tag arcade—Jack paid for those tickets. The guy in charge put them on the same team. That meant they fought against another team while lights swirled through the vacuum-like space, fog rolled in, and music blasted their eardrums. As they ran around the maze, firing at the other team while they tried to capture the base, Jack's doubts about Merle vanished—blown away into the game's rolling fog. Merle was really good at laser tag. He was fast, and the whole thing was such a blast that ended way too soon! Afterward, when they compared their scorecards, they discovered they had nearly the same score. Each had fired 136 shots, each hit an opponent almost 90 times, and both of them earned the rank of Cosmic Sergeant.

Minutes later, Lily and Ashley approached from the souvenir shop where Ashley'd bought a T-shirt decorated with black bears. If Merle and Jack looked enough alike to be cousins, Lily and Ashley could have been mistaken for mother and daughter. They had the same brown eyes and dark hair, although Lily's hair was straight as a ruler and Ashley's curly as a lamb's. They both wore skirts that hung below their knees and swung as they walked. Maybe that's why Yonah had liked Ashley from the start: She reminded him of his mother. And maybe that's why he was less friendly to Jack, because Jack looked something like Merle.

"I'm afraid we have to leave now," Lily told them. "I'll drive you kids back to where your parents are, and then Merle and I will go to the hospital to see Arlene. After that I need to get back home in time to put the turkey in the oven, because dinner shouldn't be too late tonight. Tomorrow's a school day." Merle groaned at that reminder as Lily added, "I'll get the car out of the parking lot. You kids meet me out front."

"Wait, I'll go with you," Ashley told her.

As Jack and Merle wandered toward the entrance, studying every number on their complex laser tag scorecards, an older man wearing plaid shorts and a "Save the Hemlocks" sweatshirt accidentally bumped into Jack.

"Sorry," he said. Then, peering at Merle through his bifocals, the man asked, "Aren't you the kid who was up at Chimneys picnic area last night?"

"No," Merle answered abruptly.

"I recognize you," the man said. "You were up there with—"

"You're wrong. I was here in town. Excuse me, my ride's waiting." Merle practically sprinted toward the exit, with Jack trying to keep up. They reached the curb and had to wait several minutes before Lily pulled up in her car.

"Crazy guy," Merle was muttering while they waited. "He needs better glasses."

A tiny doubt tried to creep once more into Jack's mind. Why had Merle run like that? But he brushed it aside— he'd had a great time with Merle. He was a good kid. Yonah had to be delusional to suspect him of any crime.

On the way back they joked around in the back seat, imagining crazy pictures Jack would be able to make with the one he'd just taken of Ashley. Then Merle invented song titles he could change: "Five Hundred Miles Away from Home (And I'm Out of Gas)", or "Country Roads (Full of Cow Pies)."

"You do art, I do music," Merle said. "We're creators."

Lily dropped off Jack and Ashley at Park Headquarters, telling them they'd find their parents in the conference room upstairs. When they got there, they saw Steven, Olivia, Kip, and Blue standing around a table that was spread with printed reports and photographs, although they didn't seem to be Steven's photographs.

"We have at least 30 different species of salamanders in this national park," Kip was saying. "That's more than anywhere else. They call our park the Salamander Capital of the World."

"Maybe the bears are eating salamanders," Blue joked, and then he saw Jack and Ashley. "Oh, hi, kids. Come on in. This is interesting—you might learn something."

Olivia explained that they were now searching for anything the bears might have eaten to make them aggressive. "This park is an International Biosphere Reserve," she said. "Plants, animals, and other critters—more than 10,000 species have already been documented within the boundaries of the park, but the actual count could be more like 100,000 species!"

Steven added, "Right, but at the moment we are focusing on mushrooms."

"Mushrooms?" Jack exclaimed.

"Mushrooms are a long shot," Kip explained, "but we have 2,000 species of mushrooms in the park, and we certainly don't know everything about each species."

"You ever heard of magic mushrooms?" Blue asked. "Some people take them like drugs, to get high. They're also called hallucinogenic mushrooms, or psychedelic mushrooms, but on the street they're just called 'shrooms."

"Are they illegal?" Ashley asked.

"Sure! They're bad stuff," Steven answered. "People who use them get delusional. They see things that aren't really there, or hear things, and in a few cases, they will become aggressive."

Kip cut in, "We don't really know what psychedelic mushrooms might do to bears. Maybe nothing at all.

But we're exploring the data—that's what science is all about. So let's look at these pictures once more."

As the adults focused again on the materials lying on the table, Jack drifted closer, wanting to get a look. Kip was pointing to a photograph as he said, "Here's a plentiful growth of mushrooms, and it looks like it's been disturbed. But I don't think bears did it. Seems more like some visitor gathered a bunch of them, probably to put on her pizza—a dangerous thing to do, because you don't know which mushrooms are poisonous. In this magnification, you can see that they were cut off at the stems with a knife."

"Where was that photo taken?" Olivia asked.

"Chimneys picnic area," Kip answered.

Jack froze. Chimneys picnic area. Where the stranger in the "Save the Hemlocks" sweatshirt said he saw Merle. Merle...and mushrooms? Yonah hinted that Merle was doing something illegal. Selling psychedelic mushrooms would be against the law, for sure.

"I think I'll go over to the bookstore," Jack announced. He wanted out of that conference room, away from any more talk about magic mushrooms. He had to think.

"I'll go with you," Ashley told him, "to see if I can find a Cherokee legend. Yonah said there might be one in the bookstore."

As they walked along a paved path between the headquarters building and the visitor center, Ashley stopped suddenly. "Look at these butterflies," she cried, pointing to a flock that clustered together on the ground, moving their blue-tipped gray wings only a little, crawling instead of flying. "Take a picture, Jack," she begged.

"I don't think so," he muttered, troubled about Merle and mushrooms.

"Why not? You have your camera—you took pictures at the Space Needle."

"Why not? Because I don't want to," he growled. "Don't be dumb, Ashley. Those butterflies are not sniffing the flowers—they're mating!"

"Shut up!" she cried. "Why are you being so mean? I heard what you said about me in the car."

"What did I say?" He'd honestly forgotten.

"You told Merle you put my face on a fish!"

He snorted. "Yeah, well, if you don't stop bugging me, I'll put your face on a wanted poster and hang it in the post office." He walked away then, leaving Ashley to find the bookstore by herself.

Dropping to the ground under a tall tree, Jack struggled to figure it all out. Was Merle a good guy or a bad guy? The man at the Space Needle said he'd seen Merle at Chimneys picnic area. Someone picked mushrooms at that picnic area, and they might have been the kind of mushrooms that made people high. Each evening, Merle biked to Gatlinburg with his guitar strapped to his back, claiming he worked as a busboy. Why the guitar?

Why did all those clues twist and slither in Jack's imagination like a bag full of snakes?

He knew why. It was because a scene from a certain movie wouldn't stop playing in his memory. That scene with police inspectors asking questions…of a famous singer getting busted for hiding drugs inside his guitar. Stop! he told himself.

But his thoughts didn't even slow down. Merle couldn't be on drugs; he acted too normal. Could Merle be dealing drugs? Not the worst kind of drugs, maybe, but magic mushrooms? That he picked himself? If he did that, why would he put them inside his guitar instead of carrying them in a plain old backpack? That didn't make sense. None of it made sense. But Jack kept wondering, if Merle was a busboy like he said he was, why did he take his guitar to work?

Too many questions! No real answers.

Later, they all gathered together around the Firekillers' dinner table, squeezed almost knee to knee because there were three Firekillers, four Landons, and Merle. Steven commented, "You're awfully quiet, Jack. What's up?"

Everyone turned to look at Jack, so he had to scramble for an answer. "Turkeys," he blurted. "I was thinking about the wild turkeys we've seen all over the park. Is this one of them?" He pointed to the platter on the table that held a beautifully browned turkey, now sliced into separate pieces. "I mean, *was* this one of them?"

"Oh, no," Blue answered quickly, holding the carving knife in his hand. "Hunting is not allowed in Great Smoky Mountains National Park. In fact, there are very few national parks where it is allowed. You can't hunt or trap wildlife at all. Not even those animals that are not native to the park, like the wild hogs that keep wandering inside our boundaries. Those hogs are dirty and hairy. They're about the same overall body size as you, Jack, and they cause a lot of damage to the park's fragile ecosystem. Sometimes we try to trap the hogs and move them onto Forest Service land, where hunting *is* allowed."

Yonah broke in, "But you kill a lot of them."

Blue nodded. "True. You gotta realize, if we find one way out in the back country, it's too hard to trap it and haul it all the way out, so we euthanize it."

"That's a polite way of saying you shoot it," Yonah commented pointedly.

"Euthanize it," Blue repeated. "Rangers go out at night in the high elevations of the park with night-vision goggles and silencer rifles. They'll stalk a wild hog that's been seen along the trail."

"And shoot it," Yonah said again.

"Recycle it back into the park," Blue said. "Because other animals eat the hog carcass—bears, coyotes, vultures, crows....When a hungry bear comes out of its den in the spring and finds a nice big wild hog carcass, the bear figures it's a gift from heaven."

Ashley interrupted, "You said a wild hog is about the same body size as Jack. Well, Jack is 120 pounds. So a bear who ate Jack all the way down to his toes—*ha ha!*—would look pretty big for this time of year, right? Like the bear in Heather's photos."

"Thanks a lot," Jack said, "for turning me into bear scat," and everyone laughed. Everyone except Merle. "But what I think my sister is trying to say," Jack continued, "is that maybe Heather's attack bear ate a hog and got fat."

"I don't think that's likely. But here's another thought," Steven offered. "What if the hog died from disease and a bear ate it? Could that affect the bear?

"Mmmm...." Blue seemed to be considering that. "Well, wild hogs do get diseases like pseudo-rabies and swine brucellosis, but we've never been aware of those or other hog diseases inside this park. Maybe a lot farther south, but not here. Anyway, I'll check with headquarters to find out whether any wild hogs have been put down recently."

The dinner-time chatter turned to other things, with everyone talking until Lily announced, "Time for dessert. Even though it's not Christmas, I baked us a Cherokee Christmas cake. My mother used to make these with hazelnuts, dates, and goat's milk, but I've modernized the recipe a bit since I can't find any goat's milk at the supermarket."

"I like it better the way you make it," Blue told her, starting to slice the cake Lily had set in front of him.

Pushing back his chair, Jack said, "Uh, could you excuse me for a minute? I need to…." He pointed in the direction of the bathroom.

"Better hurry," Merle told him, "or I might eat your piece of cake."

"Better not!" Jack wanted to get out of there while Merle was still at the table. All through dinner he'd been planning it, arguing with himself over whether he should do such a deceitful thing. Yet this was one chance to either find out the truth, or even better, to put his suspicions to rest.

Earlier, he'd seen Merle's guitar case in the hall, lying on the floor near the bathroom door. Moving quietly now, Jack picked up the guitar case and carried it into the bathroom, setting it on the sink counter. He left the door open just a little way so he could hear if anyone came.

It was an old case, the leather cracked on the outside and the red felt lining peeling away from the inside. Cautiously, he lifted the guitar out of the case, his left hand beneath the neck and his right hand supporting the bottom. Glancing up, he saw himself in the bathroom mirror, and he hated his own image. Jack the mole. Jack the sneak. Why was he doing this? If Merle was in trouble, there was nothing Jack could do to help him. Or was there?

Holding the guitar with both hands, he jiggled it a little but heard nothing. Then, after shaking it harder and still hearing nothing, he turned the guitar upside down.

"What are you doing?"

Jack jumped so hard he nearly dropped the guitar. He didn't need to turn around, because he could see in the mirror in front of him that Merle stood right outside the partly open door. Jack hadn't heard him approach.

"I know what you're doing," Merle said, his voice as cold as his steel-gray eyes. "I saw the same movie. You think I might be carrying drugs in my guitar, don't you? You think I might be dealing."

"N-not drugs," Jack stammered. "Mushrooms."

"Oh for cr—!" Merle shook his head and rolled his eyes to the ceiling. "'Shrooms. Like I'd be dealing magic mushrooms in Gatlinburg. Gatlinburg is not New York City, Jack. It's not even Nashville." Then, "Hand over that guitar. It's the only thing I have left from my father, and I don't like spies touching it."

"I'm not—" Jack began, but Merle was already putting the guitar back into the case.

Merle snapped the case shut, picked it up, and as he turned to go, he said, "I thought maybe we were gonna be friends, Jack. I was wrong."

He was halfway through the door when Jack cried, "Where do you work, Merle? Tell me where you work as a busboy."

The door slammed shut. Merle was gone.

CHAPTER SEVEN

"**Y**our mother has already left," Steven said from where he stood between the two beds. Grabbing Jack's big toe, he shook it hard to wake him.

"What?" Jack asked groggily. "What time is it?"

"It's seven-thirty, lazy boy. Time to rise and shine. You, too, Ashley."

Blinking, Ashley rolled over on one elbow. "What'd you say about Mom?"

"I said she's gone. She and Kip are on their way to the lab in Knoxville. Jack, you can use my shower. Ashley, this bathroom's all yours. Move it, kids. After you're ready, we'll have breakfast here at the hotel, and then we're going for a ride."

"With Yonah, too?" Ashley asked sleepily, and then, "Oh, I forgot. It's Monday, so he's in school."

"No, not Yonah. You're going with me and your brother, if I can drag him out of bed. Come on, guys, hustle, hustle. I'll tell you about everything over breakfast."

"Everything" turned out to be that Olivia and Kip were taking half a dozen different mushroom samples to the Knoxville lab, more than an hour away, to check them for hallucinogens. Steven, Jack, and Ashley would drive through the park, gathering information and images connected to the bear attacks.

"Like detectives," Ashley said.

"Like biologists or animal behaviorists," Steven corrected her. "Detectives study crime scenes. No crimes have been committed here, unless you consider the bears criminals."

Ashley glanced toward Jack. Again they knew what each was thinking. Yonah had hinted that Merle might be committing a crime. What kind of crime? It couldn't have anything to do with the bears—how could you commit a crime about bears? Jack gave a little nod toward Ashley, and she got the message: *Just don't mention it to Dad.*

"You be the navigator," Steven told Jack after they'd driven through the park entrance. So, while his father and sister waited in the car, Jack ran into the Sugarlands Visitor Center to pick up a park map.

"We're heading south," he told them when he got back in the car. "On Newfound Gap Road."

As the car wound back and forth around the curves of the road that climbed in altitude, they passed a sign that said "Bear Habitat. Do Not Leave Food Unattended. Regulations Enforced." And right ahead of that was a second sign with the word "Chimneys."

"Hey, slow down, Dad." Straining to get a better look, Jack saw three symbols beneath the word "Chimneys":

The one on the right showed a tent with a red line through it, meaning no overnight camping. The one in the center indicated that a trail started from somewhere nearby. And the one on the left showed a picnic table. Chimneys picnic area! The place the tourist said he'd seen Merle. "Can we stop here?" Jack asked.

"Yes, I was planning to stop," Steven told them. "There's a trail here we need to take. It leads to the site of that earlier bear encounter."

"You mean the attack on the man we saw on TV? The man that had bear-claw marks all down the front of him?" Ashley asked.

"Yes, his name's Peterson. I have to photograph the site of the attack. I shot the other ones yesterday but didn't make it to the Peterson site. There might not be much evidence left by now, but it's still worth documenting. You never know when you'll spot something useful."

Chimneys picnic area had several paved lanes where cars and even buses could park. The trees were so thick and close together that Steven warned the kids not to go so far that he couldn't see them, or at least hear them. They scrambled down the banks of a fast-flowing creek, then up a hillside, looking for the trail. Since the place was called Chimneys, Jack wondered if they might come across a broken-down chimney like the one at Merle's great-granddaddy's place. Instead, they found fresh green trees and moss-covered rocks and spring flowers in new bloom, but no chimney ruins. And after half an hour's search, no trailhead, either.

"Keep looking," Steven told them. "It's got to be here somewhere. I don't know why we can't see any signs."

"What's that over there?" Ashley asked, pointing. "Oh, gosh! There are chicken bones lying under that bush. What's the matter with people? There are plenty of garbage cans in the parking lot. What kind of person would leave food scraps on the ground to mess up this beautiful park?"

"Thoughtless, careless kinds of persons," Steven answered. "You've heard it, I know, the motto that's in every national park: 'Take away nothing but pictures; leave behind nothing but footprints.'"

"I'll put the bones in a garbage can," Jack said. As he picked them up, he saw that the leg and thigh bones were still connected, though there wasn't any meat on them. "Whoever ate here must have been really hungry. One end of this is all chewed off."

Jack managed to find a garbage can just as Steven called to him, "After you dump those bones, let me take a look at your map. I'm starting to wonder if we're in the wrong place." Wiping his hands on his jeans, Jack took the map out of his jacket and handed it to his father.

"Aha! No wonder we couldn't find it," Steven exclaimed. "This is the Chimneys picnic area. Chimney Tops Trail starts about a mile up the road."

They got back in the car. After going a very short

distance, they saw the marker for Chimney Tops trailhead. If they'd driven a little farther in the first place, they'd have found it earlier. The trail began just beyond a low rock wall bordering the parking lot, an easy, level introduction to a climb that was going to get a lot steeper. A few hundred yards past the beginning they saw another sign announcing, "Chimney Tops Trail, The View Is Worth the Climb."

"Are we going to the top?" Ashley asked.

"Not today, although it would be great if we could. Check the sign—it says the hike to the top and back takes two and a half hours. Maybe we can come again before we go home to Wyoming. But this morning, we have to examine the place where the Peterson attack happened."

The hike started off pleasantly enough, with birds chirping overhead and the butterflies Ashley loved so much fluttering nearby. They crossed a little wooden bridge, and then another one over a winding, bubbling creek.

"The attack happened farther up the trail," Steven told them. "Kip made me a sketch so I could find the place." A little later he said, "This is it."

The evidence of a scuffle was still visible. "Peterson must have fought really hard," Steven said. "According to the report, he hit the bear with rocks and a tree branch and everything he could pick up, which is what you're supposed to do. That's probably why he didn't get hurt worse than he did."

"Why'd the bear go after him?" Ashley asked.

"Food again. Mr. Peterson had a big lunch in his backpack, and the bear was trying to get it. Peterson lives in Pennsylvania, so Kip is e-mailing him Heather's pictures to ask him if the bear that attacked him was as large as Heather's bear."

"Hah! Heather's bear!" Jack exclaimed. "I bet there's no way she wants to call it Heather's bear, like she owns it."

As Steven took more pictures, Jack walked carefully around the area, studying the ground. Once again he found drops of blood, which discolored the leaves of vines that had been trampled underfoot. This time the blood was dry to his touch, but he knew it was real blood, maybe even bear blood if the guy had hit the bear hard enough. He licked his finger and touched a little of the blood on one of the leaves, capturing a red smear—a souvenir that would stay on his fingertips until he washed his hands again.

"You're weird," his sister told him. "Really weird, Jack."

"No, I'm not. Like Dad said, I'm a biologist, or maybe an animal behaviorist."

"I think I have enough pictures of this place. Let's go to the next stop," Steven said, repacking his cameras.

"Which is?" Jack asked.

"The Oconaluftee Mountain Farm Museum, pretty far south of here, but still in the park. They grind corn at an old mill near there, and Kip asked me to find out what happens to their corn after it's ground. Whether there's any connection with the mash you kids found at the still on Merle's great-granddaddy's farm."

"Former farm," Jack corrected him. "It belongs to the park now."

After they drove off again, the road continued to climb as they passed more pulloffs. Trees had been fully green at the lower elevations, yet the higher they drove, the fewer leaves they saw on branches.

Jack, read from the back of the map, "'Spring takes a long time to reach the top of the mountains. Some species of birds stay in the park year-round. In autumn, they fly from the mountain elevations into the valleys, as though they were migrating from north to south for the winter. This difference in altitude creates a difference in climate.' Hey, that's cool, Dad. The birds don't have to pack up and leave."

"Yeah, way cool. Especially when they're still here in winter and get snowed on."

"Let me see the map," Ashley told Jack. And then, "Dad, I know we're supposed to be investigating things, but we're not getting to enjoy the sights. You said we couldn't climb up to Chimney Tops, but there's another place here where the view is supposed to be fabulous. It's called Clingmans Dome. It's the highest point in the park. Can we stop there? *Please?* Can we just be tourists for a little while?"

"Well,...OK," Steven agreed reluctantly. In another ten

minutes, when they came to the markers for Clingmans Dome, Steven pulled into the parking lot. "As long as we're doing this, I might as well take pictures," he said, hoisting his camera bag over his shoulder before he locked the car. "But we need to make it fast."

"You want fast? We'll race you to the top," Ashley challenged him.

"Not fair! I'm carrying these heavy cameras."

"Your legs are longer, Dad. That evens things out," Jack told him.

Ashley and Jack took off at a run, skittering past tourists on the half-mile trail, both older tourists and young families with little kids. Since long legs were the contributing factor, Jack outran his sister, who came up panting three whole minutes behind him. After resting a very short time at the top of the path, they climbed a concrete lookout tower that was bigger than the one at the Space Needle. A sign told them they'd reached the highest point in the Smokies.

"We're in the sky!" Ashley exclaimed, raising her arms. "Where's Dad? He needs to take pictures."

"I'll take pictures," Jack told her.

"Dad's are better."

"Thanks a lot! If I had real expensive cameras like his, mine would be better, too."

By then Steven had arrived, and the three of them walked around the complete circle at the top of the tower, enjoying the view. In every direction, waves of mountain peaks rose one after the other, far into the distance.

"You can see a hundred miles from here," a stranger standing nearby said. "Or, at least you can on a clear day. When it isn't cloudy, you can see five states, but today it isn't clear enough for that."

"I don't care if I can only see three or four," Ashley whispered to Jack. "It's like an angel could fly down out of the mist onto one of those trees. This is heaven."

A marker explained that the park had been named for the mist or blue haze that surrounds the mountains, and that the Cherokee name for the area, *Sha-co-na-ge,* means "place of blue, like smoke."

Steven murmured, "This scenery is so different from the Grand Tetons out West. It's just as beautiful, but in a whole different way—trees and mist instead of snow-capped peaks. When we get back to Wyoming, I'll turn these photos into 16-by-24-inch prints. You can each have one in your room."

Reluctantly, they left the tower, with Steven following the kids on the downhill path to the car. They hadn't driven a tenth of a mile farther when Jack called out, "Hey! We're in North Carolina. We have now crossed the state line from Tennessee, but we're still in Great Smoky Mountains National Park. Dad, I found this Oconaluftee place on the map."

"OK, keep checking, so you can tell me when we're

getting close."

It was good to get out of the car again, once they reached Oconaluftee. While Steven went into the visitor center to talk to a ranger, Jack and Ashley toured farm buildings that had been moved there from other places in the Great Smoky Mountains. "This must be what Merle's granddaddy's place looked like a long time ago," Ashley said. "Or his great-granddaddy's."

"Can't see any moonshine stills around here, though," Jack joked.

A ranger showed them a short cut toward another old building called the Mingus Mill. Just as they reached the mill, a park aide started talking to a group of tourists.

"This mill operates on water power. That wooden platform—it's called a flume—carries water from the creek. The water rotates a turbine that's attached to two huge handmade blocks of granite that grind the corn. Come on inside, and you can see how it works."

As they followed the aide through the door, Jack told Ashley, "Maybe we'll find the answer ourselves to what Dad's trying to learn right now about the mash."

Inside, the walls of the old mill looked just as rough and unfinished as the outside walls. A counter stood in the middle of the floor, with plastic bags sitting at each end.

"Hey, Ashley, the labels on these bags say 'wheat flour,' and those on the bags at the other end say 'corn-meal.' And look at the stuff coming out of that grinder thing over there. It's real smooth—smooth like flour, not grainy like mash."

The aide overheard him and said, "We don't make mash, just cornmeal and flour. How'd you hear about mash?"

"Oh, a guy mentioned it." No point talking about the spilled mash or the still they'd discovered. "Come on, Ashley," he said, grabbing her hand. "We need to tell Dad about this."

They found Steven exiting the visitor center. Before he had the chance to speak, Jack announced, "No mash tie-in. They just make cornmeal here. Am I right?"

"You got it," Steven agreed.

"So now where do we go and what do we do?"

Steven motioned them to follow him to the car. Right before he unlocked the doors, he said, "We've done our sleuthing pretty quickly this morning, faster than I expected. So I've been thinking—we're almost at the southern boundary of the park. How about if we give Ashley a little treat?"

"A treat? For me?" Ashley brightened.

"For you. Take a look at Jack's map, Ashley. What's the next town, heading south?"

Jack unfolded the map to let his sister study it. "It's called Cherokee!" she answered.

"Yes. It's on the Cherokee Indian Reservation. The ranger I was just talking to mentioned that there's a Museum of the Cherokee Indian we can visit. Since you haven't found your Cherokee legend so far," Steven said, patting Ashley's shoulder, "I thought this would be a great place to look for it."

Ashley was so excited she practically dove into the car. But since Jack was hungry, he persuaded his father to stop first at a fast-food place for lunch, where Ashley kept urging them to eat faster. She didn't even finish her own burger. Wrapping the last part of it in a napkin, she shoved it into the pocket of her zip-up flannel shirt.

"That's going to make your shirt greasy and smelly," Jack told her.

"I don't care. Let's go."

The museum was less than two miles farther. After they parked and went inside, they were greeted by a guide, a Cherokee woman named Juanita.

"First I'll show you the exhibit rooms," she said, "and then we have a film."

To Ashley, and to Jack, too, this was a wonderful part of the day's trip. The museum was filled with life-size statues of Cherokee warriors and Cherokee leaders, arranged in scenes to make them look real. One scene showed richly dressed Cherokee elders greeting the arriving ships of Europeans. The scene Jack liked best was a warrior in buckskins holding up an offering to the gods.

While he was admiring that, Ashley cried, "Look— masks! Like Yonah made, but different kinds, too."

"These are masks worn by warriors from each of the

seven Cherokee clans," Juanita explained. "The Bird clan, Wolf clan, Wild Potato clan, Paint clan, Long Hair clan, Deer clan, and Blue clan."

"Could I ask you a question?" Ashley moved closer to Juanita and began, "Yonah...uh...a friend of ours, said the Europeans came here and pushed the Cherokee people out of the Smokies. Can you tell me what kind of Europeans they were?" Jack knew Ashley was thinking about their own Italian grandparents. She'd inherited her dark eyes and hair from them.

"Way back in the 18th century," Juanita answered, "the English and Scotch-Irish first came to these parts. A century later, they had moved onto much of the Cherokee land."

Jack, whose blond hair and blue eyes matched Steven's, whispered, "Was that us, Dad?"

Steven whispered back, "Yep. Those Scotch-Irish and English folks, the ones who chased away the Cherokees, were our long-ago ancestors. I know you're not proud of what they did, and neither am I."

Juanita had moved ahead of them so she didn't hear that—not that it would have mattered, probably. Turning around, she invited them, "If you'd like to come here into this small movie theater, you'll be able to watch the history of the Cherokee Nation on film."

That was when the Trail of Tears came to life for all of them, the story of the Cherokee people forced off their land, pushed away by soldiers on horseback. There were scenes of women carrying babies across cold rushing streams, of children shivering as snow blew in swirls around them. Then a deep, halting voice, one that sounded as though it belonged to an ancient Cherokee man, spoke the words slowly:

Long time we travel on way to new land.
People feel bad. Women cry and make sad wails.
Children cry, and many men cry, and all look sad
like when friends die.
But they say nothing, just put heads down, keep
on go toward west.
Many days pass. People die very much.
People sometimes say I look like I never smile.
But no man has laugh left after he's marched over
long trail.

As they came out of the theater, Jack saw a real trail of tears on Ashley's cheeks. She'd found her Cherokee legend, a sad one, but true.

CHAPTER EIGHT

The front door was open, so Jack and Ashley walked right into the Firekiller house. They must have startled Yonah because he whirled to face them, his right hand behind his back.

"Where's your mom and dad?" Yonah demanded.

Startled by Yonah's intensity, Ashley stammered, "Mom called Dad on the cell phone..."

Jack broke in, "The manager of a hotel near the town dump saw some bears there. Dad dropped us off. He's gone to meet Mom and take pictures. OK?"

"OK."

"So what are you hiding?" Jack came right out and asked him.

Yonah scowled, then slowly brought his hand out in front of him. He was holding a fresh, crisp $50-bill. In a rush he explained, "My mom's working late. She said there's leftover turkey in the fridge, and I should get it out and make sandwiches for us. But Merle's books were on the kitchen table, and when I moved them, this fell out of his biology book. So—what do you think it means?"

"It means he got paid," Jack answered. "He has a job as a bus—" His words faltered.

"Not at the Sunset Grill, or any other restaurant, I don't think. When people get paid in cash like this, it's from some shady operation."

Ashley sighed. "You're so suspicious, Yonah. Did you ever just come out and ask Merle where he works?"

Yonah shrugged. "What's the point? He'd lie to me. But hey, here's what I'm thinking. Here's the plan. We'll drive to Gatlinburg and go up one street after another 'til we see that red bike. It's about a thousand years old, so no one else will have a bike like that anywhere in the city."

"You're going to drive us?" Jack asked uncertainly. This would be a much longer drive than going two blocks for a burger. Their dad would not like it one bit.

"You scared?" Yonah asked, opening his eyes wide in mock fear. "I could maybe get you a car seat for babies."

That did it! After that slam, if Yonah had dared Jack to leap off the Space Needle, Jack would have take the dare. In an hour or two his parents would come back here, expecting them to be at the Firekillers', and they'd freak out because their kids wouldn't be around. But it would be worth any consequences to shove Yonah's sneer down his throat, and maybe at the same time prove Merle's innocence. If he *was* innocent.

"Let's get in the car," Jack said, his voice gruff.

Yonah asked Ashley to sit in front because he said she was great at noticing things—just one more put-down for Jack, who crouched forward in the back staring intently at the streets of Gatlinburg. He made a personal vow to be first to spot that red bike. They passed the Book Warehouse in the Mountain Mall, a Subway sandwich shop, which reminded Jack how hungry he was, Ripley's Aquarium, and then—

"Over there," Jack cried out, pointing to the right. "I don't see Merle, but there's his bike. It's leaning against a wall behind that small bus." It was the bus he'd noticed two nights earlier when they'd walked back from the Sunset Grill—the one with "Smokies Touring Service" painted on the sides.

"I'm pulling over." Yonah drove up an incline and stopped behind a restaurant directly across the street from where the red bike was parked. "Everybody out. We'll sit on the wall in front of this place. It's higher than the street, so we'll get a real good view of whatever's happening over there."

With Yonah issuing orders like a drill sergeant, the three of them positioned themselves on the stone wall. Legs dangling, they focused on the parking lot across the street and on Merle's bike.

Nothing happened. Ten minutes passed. Where was Merle? Ten more minutes, then another five minutes.

"Could we get something to eat? Maybe in this restaurant behind us?" Ashley asked softly.

Jack was hungry, too. Hours had passed since their lunch in Cherokee. "We could sit at a table next to a window in there," he suggested. "That way we can keep looking across the street."

"This place is too expensive," Yonah told them, "unless you've got about 50 bucks on you…" His words trailed off then because all of them thought about that $50-bill Yonah had carefully returned to Merle's biology book. "Here's a better idea. We'll drive to Charlie's Chicken Shack and order at the drive-through. It's just a couple of blocks from here."

"Somebody needs to stay here to keep watch," Jack told him.

Ashley shifted on the stone wall. "You guys go. I'll stay and watch."

"Maybe…," Jack hesitated. Was it safe to leave his sister alone in a strange city? What if someone…

"Jack," she mocked, reading his expression, "it's still daylight! There are people all around. No one is going to kidnap me. If anyone tries to touch me, I'll scream bloody murder. So go! I'm hungry enough to eat any kind of chicken, even fried chicken bladders. Do chickens have bladders?"

Yonah laughed at that all the way back to the car. He seemed to think Ashley was hilarious. "Get in!" he ordered Jack, starting the car before Jack was all the way through the door. Yonah obviously knew his way around Gatlinburg, taking the back streets and coming out onto the main drag right at the sixth stoplight.

They had to wait in line at the drive-through window. Jack checked out the menu—chicken bits, spicy chicken wings—but before he had a chance to order, Yonah told the girl at the window, "Three chicken strip wraps, three onion rings, three cherry slushies, and a whole lot of napkins." Turning to Jack, he asked, "Got ten bucks? That'll cover yours and Ashley's."

Jack had the urge to argue that if he was going to pay for his own food, he should be allowed to choose it, but the girl had already left the window. Maybe Yonah thought he had authority to take charge because he was a high school junior, and Jack wasn't quite out of middle school. But older did not necessarily equal smarter, Jack thought resentfully.

"Drive ahead to the next window," a voice instructed them through a loud speaker. A minute later a guy wearing a black stud in one ear handed Yonah two paper bags and a cardboard tray with the slushies.

"Hold these," Yonah told Jack. "I have to drive."

They'd just pulled out of the parking lot when Yonah swerved so suddenly and so fast that Jack got thrown sideways against the door, fighting to keep the slushies from tipping sideways. "What are you doing?" he yelled.

After pulling into a driveway, Yonah immediately cut the motor. "Shut up!" he whispered. "Look over there, at the back door of the drive-in."

And then Jack saw...Merle! So this is where he works, Jack thought. Why should this be such a big secret? Who cares if he works at a drive-in instead of a restaurant? He was about to say that when he noticed Merle loading large tubs of something or other into the trunk of someone's car, a black Town Car. "What's...?" he began.

"Weird," Yonah breathed. "Look inside that guy's trunk. There's six of those big tubs. It can't be trash because there's a dumpster at the back end of the parking lot. And now Merle's getting into the car. I'm gonna follow them."

After the black Town Car had pulled out into the street, Yonah waited for it to move all the way to the end of the block and turn the corner. Then Yonah started his own car, drove to the end of the block, and followed, staying a couple of cars behind the black one.

Somehow it was not a great surprise that the black car pulled in next to the Smokies Touring Service bus. After all, that's where they'd spotted Merle's bike. Not a surprise, but still a puzzle as the driver got out of the car, went to the tour bus, and opened the luggage bin.

Yonah parked the car where it had been before. By the time the boys joined Ashley, Merle had already begun lifting the tubs out of the Town Car's trunk. He transferred them, one by one, into the luggage bin of the bus. While all this was going on, Yonah kept staring, his black eyebrows lowered, his dark eyes focusing intently on every movement across the street.

"Can we eat now?" Ashley whispered.

"Sure, go ahead," Yonah muttered. "I ordered chicken wraps 'cause they're easy to hold. You can eat and watch at the same time."

What they saw next was one more puzzle piece: Merle wheeled his red bike inside a building and came out carrying his guitar. He climbed the steps into the bus, returning quickly without the guitar.

Minutes later they'd finished their chicken wraps, wiping their fingers on the napkins before shoving all the greasy papers into one of the bags. "My fingers smell like chicken and onions," Ashley mentioned. "Is there someplace I can wash my hands?"

"No! Don't go anywhere right now," Yonah ordered, "because if that bus moves, we have to follow it, *muy pronto!* Just do this." He rubbed his hands vigorously up and down on the front of his sweatshirt, then held them palm-up to show Ashley that they were clean—sort of.

Ashley wrinkled her nose. She wasn't about to wipe smelly onion grease on the outside of her new flannel shirt, even though earlier she'd stowed part of a hamburger in the pocket before finding a place to get rid of it. She dug through the paper bag again, found a fairly clean paper napkin, spit on it to dampen it, then carefully cleaned her fingers with it.

They didn't have long to wait before things started happening across the street. In the next quarter hour, people began to arrive, some in cars, a few in taxis. They seemed kind of old, not exactly elderly but maybe in their 50s or 60s. There were a few younger people getting on board, but no kids. And just about every person who boarded the bus was carrying a camera.

Merle helped some of the older ladies to climb on board, then he just hung around as if to make sure that everyone who was supposed to be on the bus had entered. He was the last to jump up the steps. The door closed behind him.

"Run to the car!" Yonah barked. "Run!" Jack ran. So did Ashley. Behind them, the bus drove slowly, edging into the street.

"Where do you think they're going?" Ashley asked as Yonah started the car.

Jack thought that was pretty obvious. "The bus says Smokies Touring Service. They'll be touring the park."

"Right, for once," Yonah remarked.

On the two-mile drive from Gatlinburg to Sugarlands Visitor Center, Yonah drove cautiously, staying a few cars behind the tour bus. When they reached Newfound Gap Road, the bus was only a tenth of a mile ahead of them.

Mile markers lined the side of the road. Jack knew that just past mile-marker 4 they'd come to Chimneys picnic area. Sure enough, that's where the bus slowed. Even though Yonah had stopped farther back along the side of the road, Jack could see Merle jumping out of the bus to unlock a chain stretched across the entrance. Driving through, the bus turned into the parking lot.

Yonah pulled ahead and kept on driving past the entrance. "Why aren't we stopping?" Ashley asked him.

"'Cause they'd see us." He drove around one more bend in the road before he pulled over to the shoulder. After a couple of cars went by, he made a U-turn so he was headed back toward Chimneys picnic area. Two hundred yards before the picnic grounds turnoff, he parked the car as far off the side of the road as he could without running into a tree. "Everybody out," he said. "Stay in the shadows."

"Why are we sneaking?" Ashley asked.

"If I'm right," Yonah told her, "it will be obvious pretty soon."

They crept forward like an Indian scouting party—very appropriate, Jack thought—with Yonah in the lead, then Ashley, then Jack, through forest that looked dimmer now that the sun was sinking beneath the tops of the trees. They could see that the concrete-paved parking lot was totally empty—no cars and no bus. So where had the bus disappeared to?

Wordlessly, they followed Yonah, who steered them through the forest to the farthest edge of the parking lot. A pavilion set back among the trees was empty. In fact, the whole place was eerily deserted. They must have made a mistake—there was no tour bus here. Could it have driven out from some other exit and gone somewhere else? But how could they have missed that?

Yonah swung around in a half circle and gestured for them to follow. Ahead was another gate—two metal pipes welded in a sideways *V* hung between two posts. The gate was shut, but a short chain dangled from one end, unfastened. Beyond it lay an unpaved road, with just two tire tracks in the dirt.

"This way, but stay in the trees," Yonah told them. "The bus has got to be up this road, and that's illegal because this picnic area is closed to traffic at 6 p.m. Somehow they got a key to unlock the gates."

Illegal? So this was the illegal action Merle was involved in that frosted Yonah so much! Just because the picnic area was supposed to be closed after six o'clock— was that such a big deal? A feeling of rebellion bubbled up inside Jack.

Catching up to Yonah, he started to tell him that he thought this whole thing was incredibly stupid and that they should stop right now, but suddenly, he heard voices. Jack looked straight ahead. There was the tour bus!

It had parked in front of a small concrete-block

building painted brown. The door to the building stood open, and as they watched, Merle came out of it, carrying folding chairs. He set them up on the level ground for the tourists to sit on, then went back to get more chairs.

It was a secluded spot, overgrown with foliage, bordering the same creek bank Jack and Ashley had slid along earlier in the day. After all the tourists were seated, chattering and rearranging their chairs for better views, Merle went inside the bus and returned with his guitar case. Opening it, he said a few words to the tourists that Jack couldn't quite hear. Then Merle played his guitar and began to sing.

Jack could hear him clearly now, his voice rising through branches that waved above them in the slight breeze. The song touched the darkening evening skies as the words wound into Jack's conscience:

> *When troubled times have torn the silence*
> *And hateful words give way to violence*
> *Keep still, my heart, fear not their warning*
> *For always comes the morning.*

> *When I've been scared by hopes that ended*
> *And been betrayed by those befriended*
> *I know the road will soon be turning*
> *For always comes the morning.*

Jack felt a sudden sense of shame. Merle was only a year older than Jack, a kid trying to earn some money to help his injured mother. Not even old enough to drive a car, Merle had to ride a bike to his job with his guitar strapped clumsily to his back. The only bit of luck in his recent life had been finding this job where he could sing his great songs to an audience that appreciated them. Right now the tourists were clapping and whistling and asking for more. If they weren't supposed to be in this picnic area after six o'clock, was that such a huge crime in a world full of big-time troubles? All this skulking through the trees trying to nail Merle, just because Yonah didn't like him!

It was time for Jack to stand up to Yonah. Time to stand up for his own values about what was fair and reasonable and what wasn't.

Turning around, not exactly shouting but not whispering, either, he told Yonah, "This is it! No more snarking around as if Merle's dealing 'shrooms or something! He's just singing, that's all! I'm going out there, and I'm gonna let him know we're here. We can at least give him a ride back home after he's finished."

"Wait!" Yonah's command was as powerful as his hand that clamped Jack's arm. "Look over there. Forget Merle—check out what Merle's boss is doing."

Jack's eyes followed the finger Yonah pointed toward the creek. What he saw were the chicken-filled tubs lined up along the creek bed. They must have been taken out of the bus before Jack, Ashley, and Yonah got there. Even from that distance, Jack could tell that four of the tubs had already been emptied. One was still full, and another swung from the man's hand as he climbed farther along the bank, slipping a little on the edge. The man stopped then and dumped the contents into the brush that lined the creek.

"Why'd he bring garbage all the way out here to get rid of it?" Jack asked, as Ashley peered around him so she could get a better look.

"He's not dumping garbage," Yonah answered. "Don't you see what's happening here?"

"Not really. No."

"He's bear baiting. And Merle knows that's illegal."

"He's what?" Ashley screwed up her face, unsure what those words meant.

"That guy's putting out food to attract the bears," Yonah said.

"Why is he…?"

"So the tourists can take pictures when the bears come here to eat." Yonah jerked his head toward the creek. "Like right now. Take a look!"

CHAPTER NINE

Bears. Two of them.

They didn't hurry, they ambled as though they knew where they were going and had plenty of time. Jack was struck by how much their heads resembled the heads of dogs—the long thin snouts, the same intelligence in the eyes. But when the bears opened their mouths, panting, their teeth looked a lot scarier than dog teeth.

The tourists went totally wild. They squealed, they pushed forward for position, they cut in front of one another to get a better view through their camera lenses. Merle hurried to help his boss carry the empty tubs away from the creek bed, and then he went back to pick up the picnic chairs knocked over by the tourists in their rush to see the black bears.

The bears looked big, but it was hard for Jack to tell if the bears were bigger than usual, since he didn't know how they were supposed to look at this time of year. He stood rooted, half afraid to move, although the bears were still across the creek and not too close. Then one of the bears stood up on its hind legs. As tall as a man, with the forelegs hanging limp like arms and the claws on his front feet curved inward like fingers, the bear leaned against a tree and rubbed his back on the trunk. Like a human! The second bear slipped a little on his way downhill, as awkward as a little kid trying to dance. Ashley caught her breath. She wore the same expression of wonder and fear that Jack was feeling.

As the first bear reached the base of a tree where some bait had been dumped, he licked the food once with a long pink tongue, then moved it around a bit using his front paw. Apparently satisfied, he snarfed some of the chicken and began to chomp it. Chewing open-mouthed, he stared across the creek—right at them! At Jack, Ashley, and Yonah!

On the near side of the creek, Merle's boss spoke softly through a small bullhorn, warning the tourists, "Don't get too close, folks. Stay up here away from the creek bank. If you slipped and fell into the water, that might scare away the bears. You're paying good money to see them, so be careful. You can get great pictures from right where you are."

Merle held his guitar by the neck with his left hand while he supported a frail looking woman who clutched his right arm. The woman burst into laughter, along with the other tourists, as the second bear stopped eating for about ten seconds to scratch his ear with his hind paw.

"Behind you!" Yonah said suddenly.

It took a minute for Jack to register the scene. Black bears—four of them by Jack's count—ambled into the clearing with their pigeon-toed walk. They moved slowly, turning a bit from side to side as they sniffed the air, then snuffled the ground, while moving downhill toward the food that had been strewn next to the creek.

Suddenly, one of these new bears seemed to sense the three humans standing among the trees. He looked straight at Jack and panted a little, his teeth very white against his black face. As the lead bear snapped his jaws, lowered his head, and flattened his ears, the other bears came alert to the nearby presence of humans. They growled and made *whooshing* sounds to show their irritation, their big heads turning as they stared from Jack to Yonah to Ashley and back again.

Fear rooted Jack to the spot. His mind flashed with the images of Heather and her wound and the blood that had seeped into the ground, deep red in the grass. There, right ahead of him, he saw those powerful white teeth that could rip through flesh as though it were tissue paper.

"Don't move!" Yonah commanded. "Act like you're not scared, and they'll leave us alone."

A low growl, guttural and deep, came from the largest of the bears. Reflecting the dying sunlight, his eyes glowed like bits of gold. Rearing up on his hind legs, the bear stood upright. Jack gasped at the size of it.

"Don't panic," Yonah ordered, but fear rose from Jack's stomach, jamming his throat until he could hardly breathe.

"There're so many!" Ashley gasped. Just then a fifth bear appeared, smaller than the others but moving more quickly toward them. Her voice shaking, Ashley said, "Yonah, are you sure that's right? That we should stay here and not move? Shouldn't we run away?"

His sister's voice jolted Jack into action. "He's wrong. We've got to get out of here. Fast!" he commanded. "Away from the stream. Walk—don't run."

Yonah yelled, "No! Stand still and make yourself look big! Show you're not scared of them."

"Be bear food if you want to," Jack shouted back. "I'm taking my sister out of here. Come on, Ashley!"

Torn between what he believed was right and yet wanting to protect his friends, Yonah hesitated, then decided to follow them.

The trees were deep in shadow, like pools of ink, but patches of sunlight remained where the tourists were gathered. Fighting the impulse to run, Jack moved into the open, toward them. He wanted to get where other people were. Closer...closer...they were going to make it.

Ahead, the tourists waved their arms. Some of them cupped their hands around their mouths, calling out something, but Jack couldn't make out their words.

"What?" he shouted.

"Back!" a deep voice was yelling. "Turn around!"

NIGHT OF THE BLACK BEAR

"What are they saying?" Ashley cried.

"I don't know," Jack answered.

Glancing backward, Jack suddenly realized what everyone was hollering about. Three more bears were coming down another slope. Eight bears! How could it be possible?

"Go the other way!" Yonah yelled at Jack, grabbing Ashley's arm.

As Jack whirled around, his voice froze in his throat. Black bears were coming at them from every direction— large bears, small bears, bears pawing the ground and swatting the tree branches, bears huffing, growling, and chomping their teeth—always moving toward them.

In minutes they would be surrounded with no way out!

"Ashley, climb this tree. Right now! And stay there!" Jack ordered her. For once Ashley obeyed him, letting him boost her foot with his hands since the lowest branch was higher than she could reach. That left Jack and Yonah on the ground, Jack tingling from anxiety as he locked eyes with the nearest bear across the 50 yards that separated them.

"Over here! Come near us! Get closer!" the tourists were shouting,

"No, don't go! Don't leave me here in the tree by myself!" Ashley pleaded.

"No way!" Jack assured her, his eyes riveted on the biggest bear.

Snapping its jaws, lowering its head, flattening its ears, the bear growled and slapped the ground to show his irritation. He looked from Jack and Yonah to the cluster of tourists as if deciding which would be the biggest nuisance in keeping him from getting where he wanted to go.

For Jack, it was as if time had stopped, as if his breathing might never begin again. This time Yonah didn't order him to make noise because Yonah was silent, too. The other bears came a little closer but seemed to be deciding which was more important: the humans or the chicken pieces on the creek banks. Most of them decided in favor of the chicken.

Then, suddenly, the near bear charged. "Whoa!" Jack yelled, because it was charging right at them!

"Jack!" Ashley screamed, terrified for her brother.

"He's bluffing," Yonah said, and sure enough the bear stopped after a mere ten feet. He pawed the ground, huffing, pacing first toward the tourists and then circling back toward Jack and Yonah.

"Grab that branch," Yonah told Jack, pointing to a good-size limb lying on the ground. "If he runs over here, start hitting him with the branch. But keep looking around—make sure you know where the other bears are." Yonah unzipped his sweatshirt, grabbed the two sides, then raised his hands high, stretching the shirt between his arms.

"What are you doing?" Jack yelled.

"Making myself look bigger to scare them off."
Pumping his arms so that the sweatshirt flapped between them, Yonah yelled some Cherokee words at the bear.

"Ashley, shake those tree branches as hard as you can," Yonah told her. "Make a whole lot of noise. Act like you're a mountain lion or something."

None of it worked. The big bear decided to take action. With frightening speed, he came rushing—not toward the tourists, but toward Yonah, reaching him faster than Jack thought possible. Ashley yelled as Jack started to swat the bear with the branch. That was useless, because the bear swatted back—but not at Jack. Sweeping his paw with those curved claws in a powerful arc, he sliced through the sleeve of Yonah's sweatshirt, leaving four parallel scratches across his arm.

Yonah tried to hit back, but his arms got tangled in the sleeves of his sweatshirt. The tourists shouted at the tops of their lungs, Ashley shrieked, and Jack hollered as he kept swatting the moving bear with the branch, but nothing helped. The bear's mouth opened wide, and he lunged toward Yonah's face.

In the wild confusion, Jack hadn't noticed Merle racing across the ground toward them. But suddenly, there he was, his guitar raised above the bear's head. The guitar made an odd thudding, vibrating noise as Merle hit it against that big male bear, beating him on the head with it and across the back and on the shoulders and chest until the sound became a loud *c-r-ack,* as the back of the guitar broke in half, crosswise. Merle kept hitting. Next, the front of the guitar splintered, sending bits of wood flying everywhere.

Now the bear turned toward Merle, its jaws wide, the long canine teeth gleaming. Still Merle swung at him, using all that was left of his guitar—the neck with the fingerboard. The guitar strings dangled and whirled crazily as he smacked the bear's snout with it. When the bear lunged, Merle shoved the neck of the guitar sideways into the wide open mouth, and the bear clamped down on it.

The scene suddenly turned so crazy that Jack couldn't tell what was happening. Out of nowhere, Blue appeared, forcing himself between Yonah and the attack bear. And Steven—where had he come from?—grabbed the branch from Jack's hands and started whapping the other bears that milled around, way too close.

"Ashley, stay up in that tree!" Olivia screamed.

Kip sprinted across to the man in charge of the tour, grabbed the bullhorn from his hand, and started bellowing into it, "Go! Get gone! Get out of here, bears!"

He must have turned the bullhorn to full volume, because his amplified yelling echoed so loudly it not only scared the bears, it made the whole scene feel like a nightmare or a horror movie. "Go! Get away! Scat!"

The bears decided that was enough. With the neck of the guitar still in his jaws like a dog carrying a bone, the biggest bear turned and loped away from all those shouting, screaming, panicked, excited people. The rest of the bears took their time leaving the scene, climbing the hill until they became lost in the foliage. Piles of chicken remained along the creek bank.

"I'm OK. I'm OK, Dad," Yonah kept assuring Blue. "How'd you get here? Where'd you come from?"

"Later. I gotta radio headquarters and tell every ranger on duty to come here right now. Who brought these park visitors here?"

Merle stood silent, breathing quickly, a large flat piece from his ruined guitar in his hand.

Steven was calling, "It's safe to come out of the tree now, Ashley," as he reached up to help her.

"Are you hurt, Jack?" Olivia cried.

"No, I'm fine. Just scared."

"How'd these visitors get here?" Blue demanded again.

Yonah panted, "Some guy from Gatlinburg brought them. I can't see him now. He's gone." After a glance toward Merle, Yonah asked Blue, "Hey Dad, do you have a handkerchief or something I can wrap around these scratches? They're bleeding."

"Right. Let me look at that. Olivia, will you tell Kip to find the guy who brought the visitors here, wherever he is? And tell Kip to get names and addresses from the visitors. We'll need witnesses."

Merle's body seemed to slump as though the air had

been let out of it. His gaze sank to the ground.

"And Steven," Blue added, "why don't you get your kids into your car right now, and I'll take Yonah in the patrol car."

Yonah stammered, "Uh…what about Merle?"

Was it happening? Was Yonah going to accuse Merle right here and now? How could he do such a thing, after Merle had kept him from getting his face chewed off! Expecting the worse, Merle stood unmoving, his knuckles white as he clutched a piece of his broken guitar.

"I mean, I want Merle to ride with us, Dad." Turning to Merle, Yonah said, "I owe you big time, brother. You saved my skin. I feel awful about your guitar."

"It's OK," Merle muttered, looking relieved.

So Yonah was finally on Merle's side. But even if they all stayed silent, Merle would find himself in trouble because of the witnesses. It was just a question of how much trouble.

CHAPTER TEN

Tuesday 9:45 a.m., Park Headquarters.

The table seemed about the same size as the one in the teachers' lunchroom at Jack's school, but instead of middle school teachers chattering over lunches they'd brought from home, the eight people around this table sat in silence. No coffee cups, no glasses of water—the scene resembled interrogation rooms on TV crime dramas. Merle and Yonah had been allowed to miss school to take part in this meeting, but they looked like they'd rather be anywhere else but here.

Were they seated that way on purpose? Jack wondered. The four adults were on one side: Kip Delaney, Blue Firekiller, and Olivia and Steven Landon, in that order. And on the other side of the table, in the same order, Merle, Yonah, Ashley, and Jack. The trouble with this picture was that Yonah, Ashley, and Jack had parental support directly across from them, while Merle, the kid in trouble, was on his own. And pretty scared.

Jack drummed his fingers on the table and then

stopped, because it sounded too loud in the stillness. Across the table, Kip concentrated as he shuffled some reports in a pile in front of him. Then he peered over his reading glasses, cleared his throat, and began speaking.

"Well, first I'll tell you that we got the guy. A couple of rangers drove the tourists back to where they first boarded the bus in Gatlinburg. The tourists gave us the name of the man who was running these tours—Orson Moffett. In fact, those folks just wouldn't stop talking about the whole experience." Kip paused, then smiled a little. "By the time I got there, they'd downloaded about a million pictures onto their laptops, and they made me look at all of them. Video, too!"

Merle slumped so far he nearly slid out of his chair. Even if he'd wanted to, there was no way now he could deny he'd been part of the Smokies Touring Service bear excursion.

Kip continued, "Moffett's in trouble because he didn't have a permit for commercial activity in the park. That's the small stuff." Looking up, Kip added, "The big stuff is that there's a law against feeding, harassing, or disturbing the park's bears. A federal law."

He handed one of the papers to Blue, who passed it to Olivia, who read it quickly and gave it to Steven. With his expression turning serious after he read it, Steven slid it across the table to Jack.

At the top of the page it said:

Don't Feed the Bears Act
108th CONGRESS
1st Session
H. R. 1472
The Secretary of the Interior shall enforce
the regulatory prohibition against the feeding of
wildlife on National Park System lands
to prohibit individuals from intentionally
feeding bears for the purpose of enticing bears
to a particular area, a practice known as bear baiting.

There was more, but Ashley tugged the paper from Jack's fingers. Anyway, he'd seen enough.

"A little background here," Kip was saying. "I'm going to explain the three different bear behaviors in this park. First, there's wild behavior. Bears that have wild behavior rarely ever come near people. If they smell humans, they run away from them because they're afraid of people—that's why park visitors usually don't see many bears. And we work very hard to keep it that way."

Kip was speaking to all of them, but Merle hung his head as if the words were arrows aimed right at his heart.

"The bears' number one defense against humans is their fear of people," Kip continued. "When we strip that fear away from them, it puts not just peoples' lives in jeopardy, but also the bears' lives."

Ashley pushed the paper showing the federal law

toward Yonah, who reached forward to take it. He jerked back fast, his lips forming a silent "Ow!" as the table's sharp edge stung his bandaged arm.

"The second behavior," Kip went on, "is called habituated behavior. That's about bears feeding near picnic areas or trails where they find food that people have dropped or otherwise left behind. The food still smells like humans and that would normally scare them off, but they get over their fear pretty quickly because the food rewards them."

"And speaking of food," Steven said, staring at his daughter, "as I recall, you had a half-eaten hamburger in your pocket yesterday, Ashley."

"No I didn't. I threw it away—after a while."

Jack, Ashley, Yonah—all three of them had had the smell of food on their clothes the night before from wiping greasy fingers on their shirts and jeans.

Kip added, "I suspect last night's attack at Chimneys had more to do with the third level—food-conditioned bears. That means that when bears become so used to getting human food, they start to depend on it. We found out that Orson Moffett has been feeding bears at Chimneys since the first spring thaw."

For the first time Merle spoke up. "I only started working for him a week ago," he said in a shaky voice.

Ignoring that, Blue explained, "You can't say every bear that's food-conditioned is gonna attack somebody, but you sure can't say if you food-condition a bear it's *not* gonna attack somebody. Moffett has made big trouble for us. And for the bears."

Silence. Jack felt bad enough, but Merle looked like he was ready to fall to his knees and beg for mercy.

"In those pictures from last night," Blue said, "I saw tubs labeled Charlie's Chicken Shack. When I checked with the Shack manager, he told me Moffett's been buying leftover chicken and chicken parts there regularly, paying $100 a tub."

"That's a lot of money!" Jack exclaimed.

"Humph!" Blue snorted. "That's negligible, compared to what he was earning. He had 18 tourists in the bus last night at $200 a person."

"Two hundred dollars!" Quickly Jack did the math. $3,600 minus $600 for chicken parts—that was a big profit for one night's work.

"He paid me $50 for singing," Merle said. "Fifty dollars each time I went with the tour bus people." Then, more softly, "How much trouble am I in?"

Blue didn't answer directly. Instead, he said, "I'd like you kids to wait in the hall while we have a little meeting here."

Yonah asked, "Including me? And Merle?"

"'Kids' includes you and Merle," Kip told him.

Jack looked toward his parents, who didn't return the look because they were talking quietly to each other.

As the four "kids" filed out of the room into the hall, they heard the door close firmly behind them. There was nothing in the hall but four chairs, a wastebasket, and a copy machine. As each of them picked out a chair to sit on, Jack felt the way he had when he'd been sent to the principal's office for firing off potato nuggets in a cafeteria food fight in sixth grade.

Ashley broke the silence. "Jack and I are grounded for the rest of the month."

"Why?" Merle asked.

"For going off in the car with Yonah and not telling anyone," she answered. "What about you, Yonah?"

"My driver's license has been suspended—by my parents. If I don't do anything wrong between now and the first of June, they might let me drive a date to the junior prom. But that's conditional. I'm allowed to appeal."

It was a relief to talk about it. Jack hadn't been alone with Merle and Yonah since the bear attack the night before. He said, "I never figured it out, and I didn't want to ask my parents last night because things were kind of… uh…tense, after we got back to the hotel. But how did they find us at Chimneys picnic area? I mean, you pulled the car way off to the side of the road, Yonah. Did they drive all over the park and just happen to notice the car?"

Yonah shook his head. "Our car has a Starfind Auto System. It's one of those communication things where if you lock yourself out of the car, you can call them and they unlock it. Or if you're in a crash, they instantly radio for help. And if your car's missing, you phone them and they find it."

"So they found us easy, then," Jack said.

"Noooo! That's one of the things my dad's maddest about. I mean, maddest at *me*. He called Starfind, and they told him he would have to report that the car was stolen. Report it to the police, and then the police would have to contact the Starfind people before they would even start to look for it! My dad knew it wasn't stolen. He already figured I had it. But he had to call the police anyway."

"Whew!" Jack could just imagine the stress in that whole process, with Steven, Olivia, and Blue informing city police about a missing car and three missing kids.

"Then, after our folks got to the car," Yonah continued, "they heard all the people yelling and screaming so they ran toward the noise. Lucky for us!"

Suddenly Jack noticed something sticking out from a corner down the hall. Something red!

"Is that your—?"

"Uh-huh," Merle nodded. "My bike. Kip found it last night when they gathered evidence in Moffett's garage. He found my guitar case, too." Merle stood up and walked to the end of the hall, then came back carrying the case. He sat down with the guitar case on his lap, the clasps toward his chest. After unsnapping them, one clasp at a time, he opened the lid very slowly and reached inside.

If he has mushrooms in there, I'm going to freak, Jack thought. Instead, Merle took out something that might have been a box, but the guitar lid hid most of it.

"Uh…," he began.

For a guy who could write great song lyrics, Merle seemed to have trouble finding words at that moment. After letting the guitar case slide gently from his knees to the floor, he stood up and carried the box to Yonah.

Yonah's eyes widened. "Chief Cherokee!"

"Take this," Merle told him. "It's yours."

Yonah reached for the box, holding it as if it were the holy grail. Now it was Yonah who couldn't find words. "Where'd it…? How'd you…?"

"I was planning to give it back to you a week ago," Merle told him, "when my mom got hurt, and I went to stay at your house. It's been in your house this whole while. But you kept raggin' on me all the time, and that made me mad. So, I just left it in a drawer. But now…."

Yonah shook his head and held out the box to Merle, saying, "I can't take it back."

"Why not?"

"My mother gave it to you. To keep."

Ashley's chair was close to Yonah's, and she reached to touch his arm. "Yonah, he wants you to have it. It's a peace offering," she murmured softly.

Hesitating for what seemed like a long time while he stared from the box to Merle and back again, Yonah finally stood up and said, "I accept this, brother. Thanks." They touched fists, sealing the treaty.

Yonah had just opened the box to show them Chief Cherokee when the door opened, and Kip called out, "Come in now, please. All of you."

With the Chief Cherokee box under his arm, Yonah followed the rest of them into the room. Blue said, "Put the guitar case over there in the corner, Merle. And you kids, sit where you were sitting earlier."

The trial is about to begin, Jack thought. Ashley bit the tip of her fingernail. What was going to happen? It was as if Kip had heard Jack's unspoken question.

"We've got big, serious problems from this point on," he began. "All those bears you saw last night are now food-conditioned, which means they'll be going after food whenever they think tourists have any. We'll try to take that bad behavior out of the bears before it gets passed on to the whole bear population."

Blue broke in, "We won't have any trouble locating the problem bears—with all those pictures and video tapes the tourists took last night, it's probably the most documented bear incident in all national park history."

At that, Merle actually blushed.

"What will you do to the bears?" Ashley asked.

Kip shuffled his papers before he answered, "What we

do with them now depends on just how food-conditioned they've become. From the bears' viewpoint, going to that picnic area and eating Moffett's bait has been a positive experience. So we have to change it into something negative. We'll go back to Chimneys and capture the bears with traps, then knock them out with drugs, ear tag them, tattoo them, pull a small tooth for aging purposes, and after they wake up again, we'll release them. And hope for the best: that they stay away from people."

"We're not going to be roughing up the bears, or beating them," Blue said. "We won't do anything too harsh to them."

"Unless…," Olivia spoke up, then left it unfinished.

"Unless they keep coming after park visitors," Kip said. "Then we would have to put them down."

Her voice trembling slightly, Ashley asked, "You mean, kill them?"

The four adults were silent, as if trying to think of the gentlest way to answer Ashley, but Yonah came right out with it.

"Yes, kill them. That's what 'put them down' means." And angrily, "What's going to happen to that bear-baiter Moffett?"

Kip answered, "We have plenty of evidence—one of the bus tourists, a Mr. Cabelli, videotaped everything that happened last night. It's enough to nail Moffett. For baiting bears and leading tours in a park for money, and operating without a permit, the maximum penalty will probably be a $5,000 fine or six months in jail. Or both. He could also get sued by the attack victims. I sure hope he at least gets some tough jail time."

Jail time! If Moffett went to jail, Merle must have been wondering, what would happen to *him?* Panicked, he looked from one person to another around the table.

"What about me?" Merle asked uncertainly.

Jack held his breath, waiting for the answer.

"Did you ever actually touch the chicken used for bait?" Blue asked.

"Well, I went to Charlie's Chicken Shack with Mr. Moffett, and I loaded the tubs in the back of his car, then I put them into the bus."

Leaning forward, staring intently into Merle's eyes, Olivia asked, "But did you ever actually dump the chicken parts on the banks of the creek at Chimneys?"

"Um...," Merle hesitated.

Oh my gosh, Jack wanted to shout to Merle, can't you see what they're trying to do? They're trying to keep you out of trouble, to save your skin! Make the right answer, Merle!

"No," Merle finally said. "I never actually dumped any chicken. I just set up the chairs and sang some songs, and then I put the chairs away again and helped clean up."

So many sighs of relief all at once must have raised the room's temperature by a whole degree.

"Honest, I feel awful bad about it," Merle told them. "*Real* bad! Maybe if I...what if I go to Chimneys picnic area and clean up everything, make sure there's not a shred of food anywhere? I could scrub all the picnic tables to get rid of the smells, and rake up the ground."

Kip answered, "That might be one way for you to try to make amends to the park. But there's also Tennessee state law to consider." After shuffling through his papers again, Kip added, "Here's a proclamation from the Tennessee Wildlife Resources about feeding black bears. Under 'Penalty' it says, 'Violation of this law is a Class C misdemeanor punishable by a fine of up to $50 and a court cost of $180.50. In addition, the punishment may involve community service.'"

A little sound came from Merle's throat, the start of a groan, although he tried to cover it up by coughing. Where was Merle going to get money to pay the fine?

Kip said, "Since you didn't actually put out the bear bait, Merle, I think community service might be a good answer."

Raising his hand, Steven suggested, "I have an idea. What about that hospital where your mother is a patient, Merle? You could go there and sing to the sick kids in the children's ward."

"I'd be more than willin', but—" Merle hung his head. "I don't have a guitar now. The songs just won't sound as good without my guitar."

Olivia murmured sympathetically, "It was your father's, wasn't it?"

Merle nodded. That guitar, the most important thing in his life after his mother, was now destroyed beyond repair.

Yonah broke the tension. "Yeah," he said. "Merle's out of a job and his mother's getting out of the hospital today and he can't go there on his bike so he needs a ride to the hospital. I'll drive you, Merle."

"No, you will not!" Blue said loudly. "Your driving privileges have been suspended, remember?"

"Oh, that's right!" Yonah grinned, faking surprise. "I guess I forgot!"

Like he'd forget that! Jack almost laughed out loud as Ashley gave him a nudge, rolling her eyes.

"Meeting's adjourned," Blue announced. "*I* will drive Merle to the hospital."

CHAPTER ELEVEN

O livia had to work on the reports with Kip and Blue, Yonah and Merle had to go back to school, and that left Steven and his kids with some hours to fill. As they walked through headquarters parking lot toward their rental car, Steven seemed to be arguing silently with himself. Then, when they reached the car, he stopped. Bouncing the keys in his hand a couple of times, he frowned and looked off into the trees. Finally he seemed to come to a decision.

"You two don't deserve this," he announced, "because you're still in huge trouble for taking off with Yonah in that car. But who knows when we'll get back to this area again. Maybe never."

Waiting for whatever was coming next, Jack and Ashley stood very still.

"So I'm going to let you have just one temporary break from being grounded," Steven told them. "Remember, it's just temporary. Come on, get in the car. Ashley in front, Jack in back."

What would this "one break" turn out to be? Jack

wondered. Pretty soon, Ashley started to bounce in the front seat the way she always did when she got excited. She must have some kind of clue. But as far as Jack could tell, they were heading back toward the hospital where Arlene Chapman was getting ready to be discharged.

Finally Ashley couldn't keep it to herself any longer. At first, she asked it so softly that Jack couldn't quite hear her, and neither did her father.

"Speak louder, please," Steven said.

At that, Ashley almost shouted, "Dollywood!"

Whoa! She turned out to be right! With Jack's own excitement building through the rest of the drive, they arrived at Dollywood and pulled into the huge parking lot. By the time they bought their tickets at the gate, Jack had begun to suspect that Steven wasn't doing this just for his kids. He was as much into it as they were.

Thus began a wild adventure that felt as though they'd stepped into a different dimension, a spinning, speeded-up world that left them breathless, scared, excited, airborne or soaked, depending on which ride they were on. The afternoon filled up with impossibly fast, upside-down tracks and instant deceleration, with rapid waterfall descents, a runaway mining train and a flooded silver mine, and demolition derby bumper cars that Ashley delighted in ramming against Jack's car.

"Break!" she cried at five o'clock. "It's time to ride

something that goes less than a hundred miles an hour."

"You're way off—it was at least 150," Jack told her.

Two hours earlier they'd left their father in a different section of the park because Steven wanted to visit milder exhibits like the blacksmith shop and the sanctuary for wild eagles. He'd given Jack the cell phone, but so far Steven hadn't called to check on them. Jack figured his dad was taking lots of pictures and had lost track of time.

"Over there!" Ashley cried. "A nice, old-fashioned merry-go-round."

It was definitely old-fashioned. Jack started to climb on board but Ashley cried, "Don't take that horse! I want it." She pointed to a beautiful white horse with a jeweled harness and a flowing blonde mane that stood straight up as though the horse had been lifted in a whirlwind.

As she climbed aboard, a park employee told her, "The kids call that horse Dolly. Want to guess why?"

Ashley smiled. "That's not hard. It has all this blonde hair. I mean, blonde mane."

"Plus the fancy jewels," the park lady added.

With the old-fashioned merry-go-round music playing loudly, it was actually kind of nice to ride around and around and look out at all the people who were pushing strollers, wiping ice cream off the faces of little kids, or shouting at their older kids to stop racing through the park. Just as Jack and Ashley left the carousel, the cell phone rang.

"I'm calling you from the Backstage Restaurant across from the fountain," Steven told Jack over the phone. "Ask one of the park people for directions, then come and meet me."

They didn't have any trouble finding the restaurant, but at first Jack couldn't see his father. He did, though, recognize Corinn, the pretty woman who'd visited Merle's mother in the hospital.

"What's happening?" he asked Corinn.

Corinn smiled her wide, pretty smile. "Lily Firekiller drove Arlene over here because she needed to sign more insurance papers, and Merle and Yonah came with them. So, we decided we would all have dinner together—sort of a "welcome back" for Arlene. She won't be able to work on the grounds for a while, but she'll be able to start in the office in a few days. Come say hi to them. They're over there."

When Jack introduced Ashley to Arlene, Ashley shook her hand cautiously, since Merle's mom looked so fragile. She had a wide strip of white tape across her nose, dark glasses to hide the bruises around her eyes, and she puffed a bit as she spoke to Merle and Yonah, who stood on either side of her chair. Minutes later, Steven appeared with Olivia and Blue, which surprised Jack—he hadn't known his mother would be coming to Dollywood.

The food was great, and Corinn made a speech about how glad they were that Arlene Chapman could be here with them tonight, how she was a cherished member of the Dollywood team, and how they wished her a complete recovery. As Jack looked around him, he wondered how Merle was feeling about being in this room where the walls were decorated with pictures of country stars like Tammy Wynette and Willie Nelson, but more to the point, where some real guitars hung on the walls, too.

Dessert was chocolate cake with icing an inch thick. After the servers had cleared the plates, Corinn stood again and began to clink her fork against the side of a glass to get everyone's attention.

"Friends," she announced, "all of you know that we're here tonight to give thanks that Arlene survived that awful car wreck. But most of you don't know that we have another life to be grateful for, also. Arlene's dear friend Lily Firekiller will tell us about that."

Merle straightened ramrod stiff in his chair as Lily stood and began to speak. "Last night, a black bear came after my son, Yonah, and two other young people, Jack and Ashley Landon. They were all in great danger."

Not expecting this, Ashley grabbed Jack's arm as Lily continued, "When the bear attacked Yonah, Merle Chapman raced to his rescue. Merle kept hitting the bear with his guitar until he drove it away. It was his daddy's guitar. It got broken to bits."

Corinn took over. "Merle, would you come up here beside me, please?"

Everyone's eyes were on Merle as he got up and joined Corinn. "A very nice lady," Corinn began, "someone the world of country music knows and loves, heard about your courageous act, Merle. And she asked me to give you this." Corinn reached beneath the table and brought out a guitar, handing it to Merle. "It's a Martin guitar, a very special one—it's called a Merle Haggard Edition. If you look between the 19th and 20th frets, you'll see Merle Haggard's signature there. The guitar belongs to you now, Merle."

"I...don't know what to say," Merle stammered.

"We don't want you to say anything," Bess called out. "We want you to sing."

"Here? Now?"

"Can't think of a better time or place," Bess assured him. "The guitar's been tuned, so it's ready to play. All you have to do is decide what you're gonna sing for us."

Merle stood with his head bowed, either choosing a song or maybe just overwhelmed by everything that had happened in the past 24 hours. When he looked up, he said, "Last night, after the bears....Well, I couldn't sleep, and a new song just sort of came into my head. I never even played it 'til now, so I don't know if I... but...well, here goes!"

His fingers deftly pressed the frets as he plucked the melody for a line or two. Then he hit some chords hard and began to sing:

You've got to look up
There's another day callin'
Stand tall 'cause you've still got a friend
Your life is much more than nothin' at all
When you know that you still
Yeah, you still
Got a good...always there for you...
Good, old friend!

Even though not that many people were gathered around the table, they made enough applause for a whole big audience—foot stomping, hand clapping, whistles, *whoo hoos,* and Arlene calling out, "That's my boy! He's gonna to be famous!"

Jack totally believed it, that Merle would be famous some day. Maybe in another dozen years—or even less—Jack might be bragging that he knew Merle Chapman, the country singer. For the next half hour everyone begged Merle to sing more songs, and he did, until Steven and Olivia said it was time for the Landons to go. They'd be returning to Wyoming in the morning.

After hugs and good-byes and promises to e-mail and stay in touch, they drove back to the hotel. Olivia told Jack and Ashley to pack right away because their flight would leave at 10 a.m. tomorrow. They'd need an early start to drive to Knoxville, return the rental car, and go through airport security.

As he stuffed his clothes into his duffel, Jack had the TV turned low. Suddenly he came alert, focused on the screen, and called, "Mom! Dad! Come here quick. You have to see this."

There she was—Greta—on Channel 12, announcing, "A resident of Gatlinburg, Orson Moffett, has been charged with illegally feeding bears in Great Smoky Mountains National Park. Feeding bears is a federal offense as well as a state and local offense."

Steven and Olivia got there in time to see a video of Moffett placing tubs of chicken alongside the creek. Jack held his breath, hoping—hard—that Merle wouldn't appear on screen. And he didn't.

Greta continued her broadcast, "Video footage recovered at Chimneys picnic area last night confirmed that the bear that attacked Heather McDonald had been food-conditioned, like other bears, by Orson Moffett. Moffett's lawyer will doubtlessly fight the charges, but the case *will* go to court."

"Good!" Steven exclaimed.

It was a brief news report, and Greta ended it with, "The mystery of the recent rash of bear attacks has been solved with the help of Dr. Olivia Landon, a wildlife veterinarian from Wyoming."

"Wow!" Olivia cried. "I forgive you, Greta, for dissing me a couple nights ago."

"Hey, Greta, what about Ashley and Jack Landon?

And Yonah and Merle?" Ashley shouted to the TV. "We're the ones who really solved the mystery."

"And for our reward? We got grounded!" Jack declared. "Is that fair? No way!"

Steven tilted his head. *"Mmm,* you've got a point."

"Does that mean we're not grounded anymore?" Ashley asked him.

"I didn't say that!" Steven threw a pillow at Ashley, who threw one back at him. Jack joined in, and it turned into a riotous pillow fight, but Olivia ducked out, saying she'd rather fight bears.

Packing finished, teeth brushed, the Landons crawled into their beds. As Jack reached to turn off the light, he noticed that Ashley was already asleep in the twin bed on the other side of the room. In the darkness, as Jack waited for sleep, Merle's song played softly in his memory, the song about friends.

Old friends, yes, but it had been great to make new friends, too.

AFTERWORD

Each year almost ten million visitors come to Great Smoky Mountains National Park to enjoy the mountains, the mist, the streams, and the history. And just about every visitor hopes to get a look at *Ursus americanus,* the black bear—the symbol of the Smokies. These bears once roamed freely across the entire American continent, but now Great Smoky Mountains National Park and nearby forests are some of their few remaining places of refuge.

We have to remind visitors to the park that bears are wild animals, with behaviors that can be unpredictable. You've probably heard the term "trash talking." Well, we do talk trash here in Great Smoky Mountains National Park, but we're talking about real trash—the food brought into the park by visitors and the garbage left behind. Food and garbage not properly secured are the sources of our biggest problem in keeping our bears wild.

It can happen this way: A wild bear first goes into Chimneys picnic area, for example, at nighttime. Bears are taught by their mothers to be afraid of people and the smell of people, but the bear has learned there's safety in darkness because people leave the picnic areas at night. The bear smells the remaining odor of fried chicken, hamburgers, and hot dogs in the picnic area—as well as the odor of people—but there's no one around.

So more bears come to the picnic area, lured by the odor of food. Food scraps left behind act as a reward for the bears that tolerate the lingering smell of people. Once they get used to finding and eating these food scraps, they are no longer scared away by the smell of humans.

Their behavior begins to change. Now the bears start to become active earlier, when there *are* people still there. If they find an unattended table with food on it, they'll jump right up on the table. At that point, the quality and the quantity of food the bears eat changes drastically. Now, instead of eating scraps, they're eating a whole meal. Their behavior has been well-rewarded.

As this happens again and again, these bears begin to appear whenever people are preparing food or eating. They arrive in the morning, when visitors are cooking breakfast, then come back at lunchtime, and again at dinnertime, when people fire up the charcoal grills. The bears will hang around after dark, searching for more food or scraps. These food-conditioned bears have begun to lose their fear of people, and this creates a dangerous situation for both the bears and the park visitors.

After we began to understand the stages in which

wild bears lose their fear of people, we realized that we needed to change their behavior and make them afraid of people again. The key to doing this was to catch them before they became food-conditioned.

We like to think of bear behavior as being similar to people behavior. For instance, you have a better chance of rehabilitating problem kids if you catch them when they're young and just stealing pencils, than if you wait until they grow up and start stealing cars or robbing banks. So, we try to work on bears when they're still at the "stealing pencils" stage by creating a negative experience for them. We capture them with a trap, use drugs to put them to sleep, and for identification purposes we put a tag on one of their ears. We also tattoo them. We'll pull a small tooth to determine how old they are, then wake them and release them right where we caught them.

If we make the negative experience far stronger than the positive experience of getting human food, we'll make the bears afraid of people again, and they won't come back for food. It's a win-win situation for us and for the bears.

It's a lot of work, but it's necessary if we're going to succeed in protecting the bear population in the park. When we find a bear with bad behavior, we deal with that animal. We only put bears down—euthanize them— when one goes into a car, a house, or a structure or becomes extremely aggressive toward our visitors.

Here are some statistics: In Great Smoky Mountains

National Park we average two bears per square mile, which comes to a total of between 1,200 and 1,500 bears in the 800-square-mile park. We only put down one or two bears a year. Most people think it's more than that, but we've succeeded in taking the bad behavior out of most of the problem bears.

Basically, bear management in the Smokies has changed from a *re*active program—one that responds to day-active bears that already have an established food-conditioned behavior—to a more *pro*active approach. This means that when we discover bears visiting picnic areas or campgrounds at night, we go after them *before* they have a chance to lose their fear of people. This bear management program has been successful.

What do we tell visitors who may encounter bears on trails or away from developed areas? We advise them that certain bears may be extremely bold in attempting to get food. Visitors must keep their distance from bears in any situation. If the animal changes its behavior—stops feeding or changes directions—you are too close! If the bear makes short runs toward you, makes loud noises, or slaps the ground, the bear is telling you that it wants more space. As a visitor, you need to understand what bears are telling you. What should you do? Back away slowly while watching the bear, but don't turn and run because this could trigger some bears to chase you.

If a bear persists in following you closely, or if it

approaches you without vocalizing or paw swatting, try changing your own direction or yield to the bear's travel route. If the bear continues to follow you, stand your ground, yell loudly, and act aggressively by waving your arms or throwing rocks or sticks. Pick up a big stick as a warning. If you are with other people, clump together to appear more threatening to the bear—there is power in numbers. Don't throw food or leave food for the bear, because this often will make the bear more persistent in getting other people's food.

If you think a bear is after your food and it makes contact with you, separate yourself from your food and back away slowly. In the extremely rare case where a bear shows no interest in your food and it comes after you, the general advice is to fight back! Do not play dead.

If you're lucky enough to view a bear in the park, watch it from a safe distance and enjoy this special treat. Enjoy *all* the wildlife in Great Smoky Mountains National Park: the flowers, trees, deer, elk, birds, and yes, those very special salamanders. Spring, summer, autumn, and winter, the park will reveal new beauty with every season.

Kim DeLozier
Supervisory Wildlife Biologist,
Great Smoky Mountains National Park

ABOUT THE AUTHORS

An award-winning mystery writer and an award-winning science writer—who are also mother and daughter—are working together on Mysteries in Our National Parks!

ALANE (LANIE) FERGUSON'S first mystery, *Show Me the Evidence,* won the Edgar Award, given by the Mystery Writers of America.

GLORIA SKURZYNSKI'S *Almost the Real Thing* won the American Institute of Physics Science Writing Award.

Lanie lives in Elizabeth, Colorado. Gloria lives in Boise, Idaho. To work together on a novel, they connect by phone, fax, and e-mail and "often forget which one of us wrote a particular line."

Gloria's e-mail: gloriabooks@qwest.net
Her Web site: www.gloriabooks.com
Lanie's e-mail: aferguson@alaneferguson.com
Her Web site: www.alaneferguson.com

Founded in 1888, the National Geographic Society is one of the largest nonprofit scientific and educational organizations in the world. It reaches more than 285 million people worldwide each month through its official journal, NATIONAL GEOGRAPHIC, and its four other magazines; the National Geographic Channel; television documentaries; radio programs; films; books; videos and DVDs; maps; and interactive media. National Geographic has funded more than 8,000 scientific research projects and supports an education program combating geographic illiteracy.

For more information,
please call 1-800-NGS LINE (647-5463) or write to the following address:

NATIONAL GEOGRAPHIC SOCIETY
1145 17th Street N.W.
Washington, D.C. 20036-4688
U.S.A.

Visit us online at: www.nationalgeographic.com/books